"Prove It."

"I don't see the necessity of proving anything at all to you, Mr. Franklin!" she said hotly.

"Marsh," he corrected. "Call me Marsh. And you're quite right, you don't need to prove anything to me. But what about to yourself?"

"I don't know what you're talking about."

Marsh Franklin reached out and stilled the hand beneath his own. The impact of his touch was jolting, and Pam's face reddened as she jerked her hand away.

"You need to prove to yourself that you're not a coward."

SONDRA STANFORD
wrote advertising copy before trying her hand at romantic fiction. Also an artist, she enjoys attending arts and crafts shows and browsing at flea markets. Sondra and her husband live happily with their two children in Corpus Christi, Texas.

Dear Reader:

Romance readers have been enthusiastic about Silhouette Special Editions for years. And that's not by accident: Special Editions were the first of their kind and continue to feature realistic stories with heightened romantic tension.

The longer stories, sophisticated style, greater sensual detail and variety that made Special Editions popular are the same elements that will make you want to read book after book.

We hope that you enjoy this Special Edition today, and will enjoy many more.

The Editors at Silhouette Books

SONDRA STANFORD
A Corner of Heaven

Silhouette Special Edition
Published by Silhouette Books New York
America's Publisher of Contemporary Romance

SILHOUETTE BOOKS, a Division of Simon & Schuster, Inc.
1230 Avenue of the Americas, New York, N.Y. 10020

Distributed by Pocket Books

ISBN: 0-671-53710-5

First Silhouette Books printing December, 1984

10 9 8 7 6 5 4 3 2 1

Map by Ray Lundgren

SILHOUETTE, SILHOUETTE SPECIAL EDITION and
colophon are registered trademarks of Simon & Schuster, Inc.

America's Publisher of Contemporary Romance

Printed in the U.S.A.

BC91

Chapter One

The interior of the small store was dim compared to the bright sunny outdoors, and Marshall Franklin paused just inside the door to allow his eyes to adjust. Slowly coming into focus were prominent displays of tackle boxes and lures, caps and baitbuckets, suntan lotion and mosquito spray. A large rack of camera film was for sale, too, no doubt for the patrons of Nye's Resort and Marina to use to record for posterity's sake all the big fish they hoped to catch.

No one was behind the counter, and while he waited for someone to appear, Marsh decided a cold beer would be in order. He was tired and stiff from the long drive from New Orleans, and thirsty besides. Doing his best to ignore the soreness in his left shoulder and the weakness in his right leg that caused him to limp slightly, he went past the grocery aisles toward the far wall, where he could see the glass doors of the refrigerated section.

When he reached the last aisle, he saw a young woman perched on a stepladder, stocking a top shelf. She bent forward, affording him an excellent view of her charmingly shaped backside, and a grin of appreciation tugged at Marsh's mouth. His eyes took their fill of a slender back covered by a white tee shirt, a delightfully curved derriere sheathed in cut-off denim shorts, and long, shapely suntanned legs.

"Nice," he drawled, sauntering toward her. "Very nice."

The woman jerked around, startled at the sound of his voice. Her arms were loaded with several boxes of rice, and suddenly the boxes slipped out of her grasp as one leg swung outward and she began to fall.

Reacting instinctively, Marsh rushed forward and caught her in his arms. Although she was slender and not really heavy, he staggered backward from the impact of her weight thrust against him. He felt a spasm shoot through his bad leg before it buckled. As he went down, the young woman came with him.

They collapsed together on the floor in a tangle of arms and legs. Marsh gritted his teeth to keep from groaning as a pain inflamed the tender muscles in his shoulder when the woman pushed against it to steady herself.

"Are you all right?" he asked as she finally extricated herself from him and rose to sit just in front of him, sucking in a deep breath.

"I think so. What about you?" She was getting to her feet now and dusting herself off with her hands.

"I'll live," Marsh said succinctly as he, too, got to his feet, but with much more care.

"It wouldn't have happened if you hadn't sneaked up behind me like a slimy Peeping Tom!" she snapped angrily.

Marsh was so amused by her colorful description of him that he laughed. "I've been called a few unflattering names in my time," he admitted, "but 'slimy' is a new one. Come to think of it, so is 'Peeping Tom.' I've never had to resort to those measures before, and besides, it hardly applies to the present situation. This is a store, isn't it, open to the public? All I did was walk inside, and there you were in a very provocative position. I just appreciated the view like any other man would've done." Slowly, his gaze journeyed down the length of her, and then he whistled softly. "The back view was quite impressive, but I have to admit the front is little short of sensational!" Full, gently rounded breasts swelled the fabric of her shirt, and though the hem of the shirt hung loose, it indented enough at the waistline to show how tiny that was before the sloping curve of her hips took over. "In fact," he added, "I'd say you're one heck of a sexy lady altogether!"

"When you've had enough of the scenery," she said with heavy sarcasm, "let me know."

Marsh returned his gaze to the appealing gaminlike face. "That might be hard to say," he retorted with a slow grin. "It's not the sort of view a man tires of very easily." His eyes frankly studied her, and automatically he took a quick mental tally of her attributes. She looked to be in her mid to late twenties, of medium height and slender build. She wore her dark brown hair short, and it fluffed around her face in a carefree manner. Usually he preferred women with longer hair, but somehow he liked it, just as he liked the captivating dust of freckles across her nose. But what he liked best about the face were her eyes. They were wide and soft and as clear a blue as the summer sky. The beauty of them was breathtaking.

Just now, however, the lovely eyes were stormy, flashing with genuine indignation. Marsh could hardly blame her for being outraged after the things he'd said. It wasn't his usual style to make such blatant, suggestive comments to a perfectly strange woman, but then again, he didn't regret it one whit. She was excessively pretty with her heightened color and burning blue glare, and he was having more fun than he'd had in a long time.

"Why don't you do me a favor," she said icily, "and drop dead?" Without waiting for a response, she turned her back on him, stooped, and began picking up the boxes of rice she'd dropped.

Marsh went to help her. "I almost did that a few months back," he said conversationally. "I decided I liked living better."

"Pity," came the curt reply.

"That depends upon your point of view, of course," he said politely.

Pamela Norris knew she was being irrational and shockingly rude to a customer, but she couldn't have stopped if she'd tried. She was sizzling with fury, and she avoided looking at the man as she accepted the boxes he handed her. He was crass and had made her acutely uncomfortable by practically undressing her with his eyes. His words and behavior were distasteful enough, but even worse was the unaccustomed heat that had flared inexplicably in her veins that brief moment she'd been pressed close to his rocklike chest. She hadn't had *that* feeling in years and she was as appalled by her own reactions as she was by the man's suggestive looks and comments. It was so shocking that it left her rather dazed.

Instead of climbing the ladder to resume her earlier task, Pam piled the boxes into a larger, corrugated box next to the wall. That done, there was nothing left but to turn and face the stranger again, reluctant though she was to do it. One couldn't cowardly stand facing a wall the rest of one's life.

She turned at last and, finding his disturbing gray eyes upon her once again, she placed a hand on her hip and cocked her head to one side. "Was there something here that you wanted?" she asked tartly.

His lips twitched. "That's a loaded question."

Pam's breath hissed between her teeth. "If you haven't come in here to conduct some legitimate business, then take your crude comments and get out before I call someone to throw you out! You may think you're funny, but I sure don't!" She couldn't stand the small confines of the area between the man, herself, and the wall. It was entirely too intimate, and she was far too aware of his powerful sexuality. She brushed past him and, with her back rigid, stalked to the front of the store and went to stand behind the relative safety of the counter.

The man took his time following her and, when he did reach the counter, he set a six-pack of cold beer on it. "I'll have this," he said mildly, just as though the altercation between them had never occurred. "Are you the manager here?" At her nod, he continued, "I also want to check in. I called last week and reserved a cabin. The name's Marshall Franklin."

Pam cringed inwardly as she turned to the desk behind the counter and searched for the right folder. *Wouldn't you know he'd have to be one of the resort guests?* she thought in dismay. It was just her luck that he'd probably be around to annoy her for several days to come.

When she found the reservation slip, her dismay grew to deep consternation. Marshall Franklin had reserved a cabin for the solid month of June! Any other time she was thrilled to have such a long-term booking, but why did it have to be this man?

Hoping her feelings didn't show, she turned back to the counter. "Yes, here it is," she said with a curt little bob of her head. "I see you want to pay with your credit card."

"That's right." Marshall Franklin tossed the plastic card onto the counter and, while he waited for her to do the paperwork, he deftly opened the carton of beer, took out a single can, and popped the top before taking a long swallow.

Pam could scarcely concentrate on what she was doing. Marshall Franklin propped one elbow on the counter and held his beer in the other hand. His entire stance was too casual, too familiar, too . . . too masculine! He acted as though he had all the time in the world to loiter and wasn't the least bit impatient to get on the water like most of the resort guests. But of course, if he were staying a month, he practically did have all the time in the world. She felt his eyes watching every move she made and was furious at how self-conscious it made her.

At last she was done. Pam handed him back his credit card, holding only the tip of it to insure there could be no accidental contact with his hand, and then slid a paper across the counter. "If you'll sign here, please?" She turned away to get the key.

She heard the door open while she located the key, and from the other side of the counter came a breezy, "Hi, Mom."

"Hi, yourself." Pam plunked the key onto the counter and asked, "Where have you been?"

Her son shrugged his bare, sunbrowned shoulders. At seven, almost eight as he kept telling her, he was tall for his age, and skinny as a stick because he stayed constantly active. Today he wore only a pair of tan shorts and a red cap on his dark head.

"Helping Gus fix the screen door on the fish-cleaning house," he replied. "Can I have a fudge ice cream?"

"May I," Pam corrected automatically. "Yes, you may." While Scotty went toward the ice cream freezer, she turned to her customer. "It's cabin number six, Mr. Franklin. Take a left at the second road you come to and it'll be on your right."

"Thanks. What do I owe you for this?" He indicated the beer.

Pam told him and slid the remainder of the six-pack into a paper bag while he counted out the amount.

"You ever been here before, Mister?" Scotty asked when he returned. His pink tongue darted out to lick the chocolate ice cream on a stick.

"Nope. This is my first time."

"I can show you around if you like," Scotty offered. He grinned engagingly, showing a gap-toothed smile.

"Now that sounds like an offer I can't refuse," the man said as he smiled down at the boy. "I bet you're the man who can give me some good fishing tips, too."

Scotty's grin widened as he nodded and launched into a few of his "tips." While the two of them were talking, Pam had her first opportunity to observe Marshall Franklin without his noticing. He was a tall, lean man, and her son seemed extremely small beside him. He was also well built, with wide shoulders, a flat, taut midsection, and narrow hips. His profile was angular and smooth. Beneath thick hair that was almost midnight black, a strong brow sloped downward to deep-set eyes. From the angle she was looking at him, she could see his eyelashes, and they seemed incredibly long and lush for a man. His nose was straight, classically cut, and his lips were neatly sculpted as though molded by an artist—narrow upper lip, full, almost sybaritic lower lip. There was no denying he was as good-looking a man as they came and, what was more, he knew it. He was probably so used to women falling for him that he had simply expected her to be one more easy conquest. She bristled at the thought.

There was one curious thing she noticed about him, though. Compared to herself and Scotty, he had an unhealthy pallor, as though he hadn't spent any time outdoors for months. If he planned to do much fishing, he was certainly going to have to be careful about protecting his skin. Not that it was any business of hers, she reminded herself caustically. In fact, it might give her the greatest of pleasure if he got burned to a crisp!

The subject of her unkindly thoughts reached for his purchase and gave her a pleasant nod. "I'd better be going while I still have my guide available," he said.

"Have a nice stay," she said from force of habit.

Franklin paused to look deeply into her eyes, and a slow grin stretched his lips. "Somehow I have a hard time believing in the sincerity of that comment, but I'll try my best, all the same."

Pam felt her face redden. Then he was gone, and her son with him. Gone over to the enemy she thought with deep annoyance.

The telephone rang just as another customer entered the store. Pam put away all thought of Marshall Franklin and returned to work.

Marsh's boots crunched across the gravel drive as he made his way toward the truck. The boy beside him was barefoot, and he danced across the rough pebbles as easily as though it were a smooth marble floor.

"Hey, that's a neat boat and motor you've got there!" Scotty exclaimed admiringly as he walked toward the trailer attached to the back of the truck. "It looks brand-new, too."

"It is," Marsh said. "Just bought it last week."

"You wanna go down to the launch now?"

Marsh shook his head. "No. I think I'd rather get settled first. I'll do it later this afternoon or maybe tomorrow morning."

"Okay," the boy said. "Follow me and I'll take you to your cabin." He darted back toward the store where his bike leaned against the wall while Marsh climbed into the cab of his truck.

A minute later they were on their way, the boy's bike flying at full speed down the dusty road while Marsh followed more slowly in his truck.

When they reached the cabin and Marsh stopped the truck and got out, he didn't immediately approach the building. He stood looking around and was well pleased with his surroundings. The rustic wooden cabin was nestled beneath the sheltering arms of tall pine trees and the air was heavy with their clean, sharp scent. Looking away from the cabin, he had an excellent view of the Toledo Bend Lake Reservoir. A number of fishing boats dotted the water and the opposite shore was a hazy blue-green. In the far distance he could see the bridge that spanned the wide body of water, linking the borders of Louisiana and Texas.

Already Marsh could feel contentment gently seeping into him like the penetrating warmth of the sun. The combination of fresh air, piney woods, and water was working some sort of magic on him. His family and good friend Dick Palmer had been right when they'd all insisted he needed such a vacation spot. A certain grimness began to drain away from him, eroding the depressing memory of the sights and smells of his long hospital stay and, later on, the confinement at his parents' home.

"Want me to help you carry your things inside, Mister?"

store. "Upstairs. We've been here since I was real little."

"I guess you make a lot of friends in a place like this. New people always coming in," Marsh observed.

"Sure. Last year I met a boy who came all the way from England. In the summer there's always lots of kids here, but there's not many in the winter. My friends from town come out to see me, though."

"I bet they enjoy going fishing with you."

"Yeah. Last week my friend Jimmy was here and we caught two dozen crappie right off the pier." Scotty, who had been moving at a half-skip, half-run, suddenly slowed as he realized his companion was not keeping up with him very well despite his long legs. He gave Marsh a keen look and asked bluntly, "What's the matter with your leg?"

"It was broken when I was in a car accident. I just got the cast off it about a week ago."

"A boy at my school broke his arm and everybody wrote on his cast. Did people write on yours?"

Marsh shook his head. "No." He suppressed a grin at the look of disappointment on the boy's face. "A lot of the time I was in the hospital, where they have to keep everything really clean," he explained.

"Why did you have to stay there?"

"Because there were a lot of other things wrong with me besides the broken leg."

"Oh." Childlike, Scotty lost interest and asked no more questions. "Here we are," he said as they reached the marina. There was a bait stand and a gas pump near the pier where the boats were docked. A couple of dozen yards farther down was the boat launch and still farther was a small building which Scotty identified as the fish-cleaning house.

As they walked out onto the pier, a boat was coming in to dock. Two men were in it, and Marsh and the boy struck up a conversation with them once the boat was securely tied to a piling. The men had had a fairly successful catch and one of them proudly exhibited a ten-pound bass for everyone's admiration.

A half hour later Marsh and Scotty headed slowly back toward the cabin. Marsh was feeling tired after such a long day and was looking forward to a rest.

Meantime, his companion kept up a stream of small talk. They passed a spot where there were several gum and pecan trees. "This is where I'm going to build a treehouse when I get enough boards," Scotty informed him. As a squirrel leaped from one tree to another, he added, "I want a gun so I can go squirrel-hunting, but Mom says it's too dangerous."

"She's right," Marsh said. "Guns are dangerous, and you're a little young yet to handle them. What are you, seven, eight?"

"Seven. I'll be eight in November." Scotty sighed. "I'm too young to hunt. I'm too young to go out in a boat by myself or camping in the woods. I can't wait till I finally get big!"

"Why can't you camp in the woods?" Marsh asked. "You look old enough for that if a grown-up goes along."

Scotty grimaced. "Mom says Gus is too old to take me and I shouldn't ask him."

"Who is Gus?"

"He works here." They had reached the cabin again, and Scotty darted ahead to retrieve his bicycle where he'd propped it against a tree. "I better be going now. See you later, Marsh."

"Sure thing, Scotty. Stop in to visit anytime."

Marsh went into the cabin, his curiosity whetted. Who was this Uncle Bob Scotty had mentioned, besides the person named Gus who was "too old" to take him camping? And where was his father? The boy hadn't mentioned him at all.

He shrugged as he went into the kitchen and began unloading the box of groceries he'd brought with him. It was just as well he hadn't indulged his curiosity and asked. The child's parents might be divorced and, like a lot of other little boys, he might no longer have a father to take him camping, help him build a treehouse or, when he was older, teach him things like hunting.

Marsh set a few cans of food on the counter, and when he did he noticed that one of the faucets was leaking. He tightened it, but the water continued to ooze out. It needed a new washer. He'd have to remember to tell someone about it.

A few minutes later, when he opened the bedroom closet door to hang away his clothes, he found that the doorknob was so loose it was about to fall off. Marsh frowned at that. It would seem, he thought as he went out to the truck and fetched a screwdriver from the toolbox behind the seat, that the owner was a bit remiss in the small maintenance jobs around the place.

He went back to the closet and fixed the doorknob himself. Then he finished storing away his clothes and, deciding he'd earned a rest, took a cold beer from the refrigerator and went out to sit in a wide wooden chair on the front porch, where he could enjoy the cool shade while he gazed at the water.

Abruptly, he grinned to himself as he remembered the scene back at the store with Scotty's mother. She'd been righteously indignant over the way he'd behaved, and yet his years of experience with the opposite sex told him that she hadn't been entirely indifferent to him as a man. Just plenty furious.

He wasn't entirely sure why he had bedeviled her the way he had. Put it down to all the months he'd been out of action, he supposed. She wasn't even his type of woman. She was as far as one could possibly imagine from the well-dressed, urban women he always went for. On top of that, she was a mother. Maybe even a wife.

Marsh's brows knitted together. He didn't like that thought, though logic dictated that it was probably the truth, even if Scotty had neglected to mention the existence of a father.

Marsh stared broodingly at the water. After one failed marriage several years ago and a very recently broken engagement, the last thing he needed in his life right now was an involvement with any woman. What he did need was to concentrate on getting back into top physical condition, see how many fish he could pull out of these waters in a month's time, and then go home and pick up his law practice again.

Setting his almost untouched beer onto the ledge, Marsh heaved himself from the chair, crossed the porch, and picked up his tackle box. He might as well rig the nylon fishing line through the rod and reel and get everything set so that by first light in the morning he'd be ready to go.

Pam removed the pork chops from the oven and scooped them from the broiler pan onto a platter. Next she took the slotted spoon and lifted the french fries from the hot oil in the skillet. She heard the front door slam, the signal that Scotty was home, and she called out, "Go wash up, pal. Almost time for supper."

"Okay," Scotty yelled back.

By the time he came into the kitchen, Pam had the food on the table.

"You know why that man named Marsh walks funny sometimes?" Scotty asked as he took his chair. "He was in a car wreck and broke his leg."

"Is that so?" Pam responded. She maintained her composure so that Scotty wouldn't see her dislike of the man.

"Uh-huh." Scotty took a sip of his milk, which left him wearing a white moustache. "He's got a brand new boat and motor that's super! I sure hope he'll take me for a ride sometime."

"You're not to ask him," Pam said sharply, much more sharply than she'd meant.

Scotty's brown eyes, replicas of his father's, grew large with surprise and hurt. It wasn't often his mother spoke to him in that tone of voice. "I wouldn't do that," he said defensively. "You told me never to ask favors from the guests."

Pam felt ashamed of herself. The man had so gotten under her skin that now she was snapping at her son. Marshall Franklin had been on her mind almost constantly since their unpleasant encounter, making her uneasy and on edge. By far, most of the guests at the resort were male, and she'd had her share of men's flirtations. She'd always been able to handle the situation in a calm, unruffled manner. Defusing amorous inclinations merely went with the territory, and she'd never given such episodes more than a passing thought. But today had been unaccountably different. She was angry at the man for stepping out of line and angrier still with herself because she couldn't forget him. Her skin warmed at the recollection of his arms clasped around her, the sensation of his hands on her arms, the strong impact on something primitive that had been buried deep within her and practically forgotten. Not since the early days of her marriage had she felt that thrill of spontaneous desire, and that it should happen with an arrogant stranger was both disgusting and frightening.

Scotty was still watching her with anxiety in his eyes. Pam went swiftly to him, ruffled his hair, and gave him a fierce hug. "I didn't mean to scold you, honey," she said soothingly. "I know you would never bother our guests like that. I guess I'm just tired and a little cranky. Still love me?" she asked with a whimsical smile.

"'Course I do." Her son flashed her a brilliant, forgiving smile, then added prosaically, "I'm hungry. Can we eat now?"

Pam served his plate and then her own, refraining from offering to help as Scotty cut his meat; he was as independent as they came and never allowed her to do anything for him that he believed he could do for himself, however awkwardly.

"When you were coming in, did you happen to notice whether Zelma had closed the store yet?" she asked as they settled down to eat.

"She's doing it now. Gus just came to pick her up," he replied. "They're going to town after supper to the Merls for homemade ice cream, and they said I could go with them if it's okay with you."

Pam smiled. "More ice cream. But I guess it's all right."

The Merls lived next door to Scotty's friend Jimmy, and he often went to play with him while the Emerys visited their friends.

Gus and Zelma Emery were more like family to Pam than employees. They had both worked for her uncle, Bob Nye, for over twenty-five years, and, after his death two years ago, had continued to work for her. Gus was the maintenance man around the place; Zelma cleaned the cabins and helped in the store. Through the past six and a half years they had watched after her and Scotty like doting grandparents and, during her uncle's illness, had helped her care for him until his death. Their home was a few miles down the road, and next year they would both be retiring. Pam knew she would miss their easy camaraderie around the resort, but it was comforting to know they would remain close by. They were the nearest thing to relatives that she had.

Of course, if her financial difficulties didn't clear up soon, there might not be any business for them to retire from, much less continue to provide a living for herself and Scotty. Pam had inherited a large amount of debt from her uncle and, though the creditors had bent over backwards to be accommodating, it seemed to her that each month it became harder and harder to stretch her money.

She mulled over the problem that evening after Scotty had left for town with the Emerys. She piled her bookkeeping records on the table as she'd done several nights in a row, but all at once she simply couldn't face it again. She practically knew the numbers by heart anyway, and no amount of creative juggling was going to change the bottom line. Nye's Resort and Marina was in serious trouble.

Needing an escape from her dismal problems, Pam let herself out of the apartment above the store, ran lightly down the outside staircase, and went toward the duck pond.

Rusty, Scotty's dog, a large orange-colored mixed breed, came ambling around the side of the building and fell into step beside her. Pam was grateful for his company.

"What am I going to do, old boy?" she asked him. "Struggle on as I'm doing, cutting every corner until it's mutilated, or go further into debt by taking out another loan? Always supposing the bank will go along with it, that is?"

Rusty replied with a cheery wag of his tail and, when they reached the pond and Pam sat down on the concrete bench on the bank, he vanished into the nearby underbrush to investigate a rustling sound.

Late afternoon shadows cast a blue-black darkness over the area, yet it felt cool and peaceful after the heat of the day. Pam enjoyed the moment of rest beneath the shade of the trees and, clasping her arms around one knee, gazed idly at the water. The ducks floated lazily as though they, too, were taking it easy after a long and busy day.

Pam's thoughts turned inward. It was strange how people's lives could turn out so differently than they had ever imagined them to be. Certainly, when she was a girl growing up in a suburb of Chicago, she had never dreamed she would someday be running a fishing resort in Louisiana. She hadn't dreamed, either, of being a single parent. Starry-eyed with infatuation she thought was love, when she became a bride at nineteen she'd expected a Cinderella kind of "happily ever after." Her own parents had divorced when she was ten, but instead of disillusioning her about marriage as an institution, it had only reinforced her determination to make her own marriage succeed.

The truth of it was that it had been a dismal failure from the start, and it seemed that the harder she had tried to make it into something good, the worse it got. Scotty was only nine months old when Mike walked out on her.

Poor Mike. Pam sighed heavily. So much for the freewheeling lifestyle he'd sought away from her. So much, too, for the dreams she'd had to create a stable and happy family life. All so many ashes. Cold, dead ashes. Before there could even be a divorce, Mike and the woman he was living with had died in a motorcycle accident.

Were everyone's dreams as unattainable as theirs had been? she wondered. One thing she did know.

Life's harsh realities had taught her it was dangerous
. . . and stupid . . . to dream.

"Good evening."

Pam jumped at the unexpected sound and twisted
around to see Marshall Franklin standing behind her.
Her heart began to pound, partly from being startled,
partly at the sight of the man who had occupied far too
much time in her thoughts all afternoon.

"Must you continually sneak up on me like that?"
she demanded in an aggrieved voice. "What are you
anyway, part Indian?"

He laughed at that. "Maybe I am. Mind if I join you,
or am I interrupting a deep train of thought? You
looked as though you were doing some pretty serious
contemplation."

"Philosophizing on the meaning of life and getting no
answers whatsoever, Mr. Franklin," Pam said as her
calm suddenly returned. "Have a seat." She waved a
hand, indicating the space beside her.

He sat down on the bench and gazed toward the
water. "Sounds like a weighty subject for so nice an
evening," he commented.

"It is. Far too weighty." Pam smiled, erasing the
somber expression from her eyes. "Tell me," she said
with polite interest, "have you gotten your line wet
yet?"

Franklin shook his head, and, when he looked at her
and smiled, Pam forgot her earlier anger toward him
and felt herself succumbing beneath the friendly
warmth of his expression. Close up like this, she had a
fascinating view of his face, of the lines across his

forehead, the crinkles around his dark eyes, of the attractive way one corner of his mouth quirked upward a bit more than the other.

"No," he said, replying to her question. "I was a little tired and decided it was better to take it easy the rest of the afternoon. I'll get an early start in the morning." With a small, almost imperceptible wince, he shifted his position, favoring his right leg.

"My son told me you'd been injured in an accident," Pam said. "I hope you're fully recovered and will be able to enjoy your vacation with us."

"Thanks. I'm fine," he answered. "I just get these twinges now and then when I overdo it or get too tired." Changing the subject, he went on, "That boy of yours is a fine young man. You must be very proud of him."

Pam nodded. "Yes. I am."

A small silence fell over them along with the gathering dusk. All at once there seemed nothing else to say, and Pam was again acutely aware of the man's overtly virile sensuality and a growing feeling of nervousness.

Finally, out of desperation for something to say, she ventured, "I hope you found your cabin satisfactory?"

"Almost," came the reply. "The doorknob on the closet was about to fall off, so I fixed it myself. And there's a leak around the kitchen faucet. Someone needs to attend to it. It's wasting money as well as water. You should be more careful about small details like that."

Stung by his criticism, valid though it might be, Pam's voice was frosty as she said, "I'll have Gus get to it first thing tomorrow, Mr. Franklin. I'm terribly sorry you were inconvenienced." She got to her feet, about to leave.

"Touchy, aren't you?" Franklin also got up, and his gaze was penetrating as he looked at her. "I wasn't exactly inconvenienced. I was merely pointing out that if the owner wants to maintain a good reputation in a business such as this, little things should be kept up as well as the larger, more obvious maintenance jobs."

"Thank you so much for advising me how to run my business," Pam snapped, thinking of poor, overworked Gus who couldn't keep up with everything that needed to be done and never complained because he knew she couldn't afford to hire more help to ease his burden. "I can't," she added with cutting sarcasm, "imagine how I ever managed before without your input!"

The skin crinkled around the man's eyes as he grinned and nodded. "Happy to be of help," he retorted cheerfully. "You know, your eyes really are gorgeous when you're riled. Blue fire. Almost makes a man want to stir you up just for the pleasure of seeing the sparks fly."

Pam stiffened. "You," she said in a low voice that quivered with fury, "are the most obnoxious person I've ever met! If you would care to leave here tomorrow and move to another resort that's better run, I'd be positively *delighted* to help you make the reservation."

"No thanks," he said offhandedly. "I sort of like this place in spite of its shortcomings." His eyes raked her as they'd done earlier that afternoon. "I'm certain none of the other places can offer such enticing side benefits as this one."

Pam clenched her fists and, with supreme effort, restrained herself from slapping the smug, offensive expression on his face.

"You'll find no benefits here, Mr. Franklin," she said with icy bluntness, "except those printed in our brochure. You're only deluding yourself if you believe otherwise."

Before she could lose what control she still had over her temper, Pam turned quickly and walked away. Quelling a strong instinct to run, she paced herself, back rigid, shoulders squared, chin high. She had too much pride to allow him to see just how seriously he had damaged her emotional equilibrium.

Chapter Two

$\mathcal{T}$he sun was high, its rays relentless as it beamed down to reflect off the open water. The searing heat penetrated the cloth of Marsh's cotton shirt, and his back was beginning to feel as though it were on fire. He decided to call it a morning.

He'd begun fishing shortly after daybreak and had done pretty well. There were four nice-sized large-mouth bass and a multitude of crappie on the stringer.

Marsh wiped his damp brow with his shirtsleeve and started the motor. Soon the boat was skimming across the water.

When the reservoir had been built, taking in what had been the Sabine River, it had also flooded much of what had once been dry land. The lake was dotted with the decaying remains of trees, stark gray poles poking upward toward the sky like guideposts. Many, however, were submerged beneath the water, treacherous to the unwary boater.

Here and there were small islands, minute splashes of green trees and cattails surrounded by water. Marsh wove his way carefully through the passes, taking his time. He felt relaxed and pleasantly tired. Fishing was a sport he'd long enjoyed, yet for the past couple of years he'd somehow gotten so busy and wrapped up in the demands of his work that he simply hadn't taken the time to indulge. Instead, he'd contented himself with an occasional game of golf or tennis and jogging a couple of miles each morning. Today he'd realized what he had been missing. The soft sigh of the water lapping against the boat, the occasional swishing sound of a nearby fish brought a quiet satisfaction he'd almost forgotten existed. Such solitude gave a man a rare chance to think.

At the dock, Marsh secured his boat and, carrying his catch, headed straight for the cleaning house. Hot, thirsty, and smelly as he felt, the job had to be done, and there was no point in putting it off.

While he worked, a gray-haired man in his sixties stopped by. "'Morning," he said affably. "Looks like you hauled in a good catch."

Marsh nodded. "I'm satisfied. Only thing," he added with a grin, "is that now I've got too many fish for just one person to eat. Care for a mess?"

"No thanks," the older man politely declined. "The missus and I got about all the fish we can eat. If I don't catch 'em myself, usually some guest like yourself keeps us supplied. Right now we've got a freezer full. I'm Gus Emery, by the way," he added. "I keep up with things around here. I thought I'd tell you I fixed that leaky faucet in your cabin."

"Thanks," Marsh said. He began filleting the fish into nice plump slices, discarding the bones. "I guess a job like yours keeps you pretty busy, doesn't it?"

Gus nodded. "Especially these past two years, since Bob Nye died. He was the owner, and we made a pretty good team keeping this place in top-notch shape, but now I have to tend to the heavier things by myself. Pam's good at running the store and doing the office work, but she's not too handy when it comes to fixing things, and neither is Zelma." At Marsh's quizzical glance, he expounded, "Zelma's my wife. She cleans the cabins and helps out Pam in the store."

"Is Pam the young woman who checked me in yesterday? Scotty's mother?"

"Yup." Gus leaned against the door frame. "Pamela Norris. Bob Nye was her uncle. He was a bachelor, and he left this place to her." He heaved a sigh. "Pam's a hard worker, but she's fighting an uphill battle trying to run this place by herself. 'Course we do all we can, Zelma and me, but she needs younger, stronger help around here, and she can't afford to hire extra people."

"Hmmm. What about her husband?" Marsh asked in spite of himself. "Doesn't he help out?"

"He died six or seven years ago," Gus said, "so it's just Pam and the boy."

"I see," Marsh said thoughtfully, digesting this piece of news.

The screen door banged loudly, announcing Scotty's arrival. "Hi," he said breezily. "How'd you do, Marsh?"

Marsh indicated the pile of fish in the pan on the counter. "See for yourself," he invited.

Gus straightened and tipped his cap brim. "Guess I better get on back to my mowing," he said, "or I won't even be half done by sundown."

"Nice talking to you," Marsh said.

"Same here. See you both later."

When the man was gone, Scotty admired Marsh's catch, chattered about some of his own catches, and added, boasting, "I bet my dad could've caught the biggest trophy-sized bass in the lake if he came here. He was a great fisherman."

"That so?" Marsh asked idly.

Scotty nodded. "My dad was good at everything. He even went moose-hunting in Alaska one time. Alaska," he explained, "is real far from here."

"I've heard." Marsh took care to hide his grin.

Scotty edged around the counter and propped one elbow on it, peering down at the growing pile of filleted fish. "You gonna eat all that by yourself?" he asked curiously.

"I was thinking about inviting you and your mom to a fish fry tonight at my cabin. What do you think?"

Scotty's eyes lit up. "Super! I'll tell Mom." He darted toward the door. "I better go now. It'll be lunchtime soon. See you tonight."

Scotty's confidence in their impromptu dinner plans did not extend to Marsh. After the angry way Pamela

Norris had left him yesterday evening, he had serious doubts about whether he'd have guests tonight.

The soft-drink delivery man found Pam restocking the magazine rack. "All I need now is your John Hancock on the order form, Pam, and I'll be on my way."

Pam quickly scribbled her name and handed back the clipboard. "See you next week, Harry."

When he was gone, Pam glanced at the clock. It was almost noon. Zelma would relieve her soon so she could take her lunch break.

Just as she lifted a fresh stack of magazines, Scotty ran into the store. "Guess what?" he greeted. "Marsh asked us to a fish fry tonight. I told him we'd come."

"*What?*" The magazines fell with a thud, but Pam ignored them as she stared at her son.

"He *invited* us, Mom. Don't you want to go?"

Pam didn't try to hide her exasperation. "You know better than to accept an invitation without checking with me first!"

Scotty scrunched his nose and shrugged his shoulders. "I forgot. Don't you want to go, Mom? Don't you like him?"

How was it a child could always zero in on what was really bothering an adult? Pam wondered. Scotty seemed to have built-in radar that could detect the truth of her feelings beneath her careful facade.

"It has nothing to do with whether I like him or not," she stated, not very truthfully. "I have work to do tonight and I don't have time to waste visiting with our guests. They're on vacation; I'm not."

Scotty's shoulders sagged with disappointment. "We have to eat supper anyway," he pointed out with maddening male logic. "I don't see why we can't eat with Marsh just as well as at home."

"Well, we can't, and that's all there is to it," Pam said decisively. She stooped to gather the haphazardly strewn magazines. "After lunch you can just march down to his cabin and tell him we can't make it. Is that understood?"

Scotty gave her an assessing look as though he were trying to gauge the extent of her displeasure. Apparently he read her expression correctly. Grimacing, he said, "Yes, ma'am, I understand."

Zelma arrived then, so Pam hastily dropped the subject. "Go on upstairs," she told Scotty, "and wash up for lunch. I'll be there in a minute."

"Okay." Scotty hurried away, eager, Pam thought wryly, to escape her wrath.

Zelma took up her position behind the counter and thrust a pencil above her ear, so that it stuck out like a yellow arrow in front and back of her thick short-cropped salt-and-pepper hair. Pink-rimmed eyeglasses perched low on the bridge of her nose, and she was forever pushing them up.

"The folks in cabin eight want to stay two more days. Do you have a vacancy for them?" she asked.

"Not in the same cabin," Pam replied. "I'm pretty sure another party reserved it for tonight. Check and see," she suggested. As Zelma opened the reservation log, she added, "Think they'd want to move to a two-bedroom?"

Zelma shrugged. "I don't know. Yes, here it is, and

you're right. Number eight is booked for tonight. The man said he'd drop into the store during the next hour. I'll offer him number four. It's the best we can do."

Pam nodded, placed the last of the magazines on the rack, and headed toward the door. "See you later. I'm going to lunch."

"All right." Slyly, Zelma added, "I hear you'll be having fish tonight."

Pam stopped dead in her tracks and whirled around. "Where did you hear that?"

"From the man in number six. I was just finishing up with his cabin when he came in. He said you and Scotty were going to have supper with him tonight."

"Well, he's mistaken," Pam said shortly. "He made his plans with Scotty, not with me, and I have no intentions of going."

"You're not really going to turn down an evening with a nice-looking man like that, are you?" Zelma scolded. "It would do you good, Pam. You hardly ever step out with a man."

"Having dinner at one of the guests' cabins is hardly what I'd call 'stepping out,' Zelma," Pam said. "Besides, I don't have time for it."

"Hmmph," Zelma grunted. "You better start making a little time in your life for men or, before you know it, you'll be over the hill and none of them will even look at you. If you're not already, someday you're going to be a very lonely woman."

Pam forced a laugh. "Maybe I'll be lonely, but at least I won't get hurt. Besides, just because I won't have dinner with Mr. Franklin doesn't mean I never accept invitations from men. You know I've gone out a few times with Andy Graham."

Zelma tossed her head derisively. "And a lot less than he'd like, too, from what I hear."

"I don't have time to discuss my love life," Pam said loftily. "Scotty's waiting for his lunch."

"Wouldn't take any time at all." Zelma had the last word before Pam could get out the door. "There's not much to discuss."

Pam slowly climbed the stairs to her apartment, trying to dismiss Zelma's comments from her mind. The trouble was, there was truth in what she'd said, much as she hated to admit it. Sometimes she was lonely. Very lonely.

At such times it did little good to comfort herself that she was a far cry from the weak, indecisive person she'd been when she'd been married to Mike. She could congratulate herself all she wanted on her independence, on her ability to take care of herself, to raise a child, to run a business—none of it helped when that certain ache lodged in her throat and she curled up, like every other night, all alone in her double bed.

Still, on the flip side of the coin was her knowledge of what marriage was really like, and Pam had no use for more of the same. Marriage, for a woman, meant being submissive, having no money of your own, no power to make decisions. It meant submerging your own needs and desires for those of another. It meant putting on a cheerful face when you felt like crying, and being hurt and bewildered and humiliated time after endless time. So what if she occasionally envied a couple who seemed to enjoy each other; so what if she felt a bit wistful over Gus and Zelma's easy companionship after forty-odd years of marriage; so what if she was the odd one out among the married couples at a P.T.A. meeting; so what if she sometimes felt incomplete and had a vague, indefinable yearning for something more in her life besides a business and a little boy? *So what?*

Irritably, Pam tugged open her apartment door. One thing she knew. She was still better off alone than she'd ever been in her marriage and, because of it, she wasn't likely ever again to get beyond a movie or a dinner date with a man.

After a shower and lunch, Marsh felt like a new man. He went out onto the screened porch, sank lazily into the lounge chair, and opened a novel. Funny how he now enjoyed an occasional book again. While he'd been in the hospital he'd been so morose over being where he was that he hadn't been able to get interested in much of anything beyond how each day dragged by so slowly with the monotonous hospital routine.

He didn't get beyond the first page, however, before Scotty clattered around the curve in the road and skidded his bike to a halt in front of the walk.

"Hi," Marsh said as the boy opened the screened door and came onto the porch. "Can I offer you a Coke?"

Scotty shook his head. "I can't stay. I came to tell you we can't come to supper tonight."

Just as he'd thought. "That's too bad," Marsh said. "Did your mother send you to tell me?"

Scotty nodded. "She said to say 'thank you,' but she has work to do tonight."

"I see. Well, maybe another time."

"Yeah." Scotty grinned. "I hope so. Hey, I like your rod and reel. Is this the one you used for the black bass?" He touched it reverently where it was propped against the wall.

Marsh nodded.

"What kind of lure did you use?"

"The artificial crawfish."

"Did you have to fish deep?"

"Around fifteen feet."

Scotty sighed. "I hardly ever get to fish for bass."

"Why is that?"

The boy shrugged his skinny shoulders. "It's too far out and Mom doesn't like to go out in the boat and I can't go by myself until I get bigger. Sometimes Gus takes me, but it doesn't happen very much."

"Maybe you can go with me some morning, then," Marsh offered.

Scotty's expression brightened. "Do you mean it?" His face quickly grew serious. "Mom says I'm never to ask the guests to take me with them."

Marsh winked. "You didn't ask," he pointed out. "I invited."

"Yeah!" A slow grin stretched across Scotty's face. "Yeah, that's right!"

After the boy had gone, Marsh considered his rejected dinner invitation. His first inclination was to let the matter drop. Scotty's mother was a difficult woman who frankly disliked him.

True, he'd brought a lot of that dislike on himself with his teasing innuendos, but still, it hardly seemed important. Just because she had a certain refreshing, natural appeal that was lacking in most women of his acquaintance and a figure that was like a magnet to his eyes were no reasons to develop an interest in her on any level. He wasn't in the mood for any complications to his life. Besides, he'd only suggested the dinner because Scotty happened to show up while he'd been cleaning the fish.

But then he changed his mind. The prospect of cooking all that fish just for himself held absolutely no appeal. Maybe he'd had too many dreary meals alone in his hospital room. Whatever the reason, a short time later Marsh found himself strolling toward the camp store.

Pamela Norris was busy waiting on several customers when he arrived, so Marsh went over to the magazine rack and began thumbing through the material there while he waited for the store to clear out.

Pam saw him enter the store and she tensed instantly. Busy as she was, in one swift glance she took in his appearance. He wore tan shorts and a white knit polo shirt, and the sheer masculinity of him assaulted her senses with a knock-out blow. His dark hair tumbled over his brow and his profile was strongly etched like a rough silhouette against the brilliant light of the sun streaming in through the storefront window. His angular body was firm and muscular and the only telltale sign of his recent injuries was that below a powerful thigh, his right leg appeared a little whiter and a little thinner than the left. But if he were self-conscious about it, he gave no sign.

It was another ten minutes before the last of the customers had been waited on, and all the while Marshall Franklin occupied himself thumbing through magazines. It was obvious to Pam that he had not come to make a purchase, but rather to speak with her, and was biding his time until it was convenient. That knowledge made her edgy, and she felt a little as though she'd been tossed to the lions when no more customers remained to protect her from his attentions.

She was annoyed with herself for feeling that way. After all, she was twenty-eight years old, not some simpering, giddy, inexperienced teenager! Why was it that this man, of all the men in the entire world, should make her feel nervous and uncertain of herself? And why did she suddenly wish, when his cool gray eyes fell upon her, that her hair was fixed in a more becoming fashion than it's breezy, swept-back style, that she'd taken time after lunch to repair her lipstick, that she was wearing something nicer than these faded jeans and a five-year-old shirt?

He came toward the counter and leaned against it in a lazy manner, as though he had all day to chat. But his relaxed demeanor belied the direct attack of his words.

"You don't have work to do tonight," he said flatly. "You're afraid to have dinner with me."

Pam gasped. "You're crazy!" she exclaimed.

"Am I?" His gaze was penetrating as he leaned across the counter so that his face was only scant inches from hers. "Then prove it by accepting my invitation."

"I don't see the necessity of proving anything at all to you, Mr. Franklin!" she said hotly.

"Marsh," he corrected. "Call me Marsh. And you're quite right, you don't need to prove anything to me. But what about to yourself?"

"I don't know what you're talking about!" Pam pulled her gaze from his and, reaching for a dust cloth, began wiping off the candy rack, an entirely unnecessary chore since it had already been done once that day.

Marshall Franklin reached out and stilled the hand beneath his own. The impact of his touch was jolting, and Pam's face reddened as she jerked her hand away.

"You need to prove to yourself that you're not a coward."

"I know I'm not!" Pam snapped. "I simply have work to do tonight."

"Liar," Marsh said softly.

Pam sucked in a ragged breath and met his gaze directly. "Look," she said as she drew herself up to her full height, "for some reason you enjoy needling me. You've done so ever since you arrived. Well, if it gives you pleasure, feel free, but that doesn't alter the fact that I have the right to avoid socializing with you. I don't like you, Mr. Franklin, and that's the gist of it."

"Is it really me you don't like," he asked in a low, silky tone, "or the fact that you're as attracted to me as I am to you? Why are you afraid of the truth?"

"It isn't the truth."

"No?" His lips parted into a sensual smile that was unnerving to her. "Then you should be able to handle having dinner with me without any fear, shouldn't you?

Especially since your son will be there also to chaperone you."

"I scarcely need a chaperone at my age!" she said, outraged.

"Ah-hah!" The smile twisted into a mocking grin. "Then you'd prefer to just have an intimate dinner for two!"

"Certainly not!" she exclaimed, scandalized that he should think she was hinting at that.

"Then a threesome it is," Marsh said. "Seven o'clock." He straightened and started moving toward the door.

"I won't be there," Pam said obstinately.

"Sure you will," he said easily, "because if you aren't, I'll tell your son he has a coward for a mother, and we don't want that, do we?"

"You leave my son out of this!" she grated harshly. "You have no right to tell him any such thing!"

"Then come to dinner and I won't." Marsh lifted his hand in a parting wave and left the store.

At a quarter to seven, Scotty skipped along beside Pam as they took the camp road that went past the marina before curving its way through the stand of pines toward the secluded cabins.

"How come we're going to eat with Marsh after all?" Scotty asked. "You said you had to work tonight."

"It gets me out of cooking supper," Pam said lightly. "Besides, I knew you wanted to go. You like Marsh a lot, don't you?"

Scotty nodded. "He said he'd take me fishing in his boat sometime, and I didn't ask him, Mom. Can I go?"

Pam smiled at her son, but her reply was noncommittal. "We'll see," she said vaguely.

When they reached the cabin, the mouth-watering aroma of frying fish wafted through the door, out to the screened porch and beyond. "Oh boy, that smells good," Scotty exclaimed. He ran ahead of Pam up the steps and opened the door of the porch. "We're here, Marsh," he yelled, exuberantly announcing their presence.

Almost at once Marsh opened the cabin door, dressed in dark slacks, a fresh sports shirt, and with a towel serving as an apron tucked into the waistband of his pants. His eyes briefly met Pam's, then his gaze went to Scotty as he gave him a warm smile.

"Come in, come in," he greeted heartily. "Excuse me while I get back to the kitchen. The fish need turning."

Pam reluctantly followed her son inside the cabin, and though Scotty went into the kitchen area, she stood on the fringes, watching as Marsh deftly turned the fish in the hot, bubbling oil.

When he was done, he looked at Pam, and, though there was a gentle teasing expression lurking in his eyes, there was also frank admiration as he took in her appearance. Pam felt her face color slightly as his gaze traveled from her freshly shampooed and curled hair, her carefully applied makeup, on down to the silky blue skirt and blouse and the neat silver sandals she wore with it.

"Nice," he said softly. "Very nice."

"Thank you." Pam hoped that the uncomfortable fluttering of her heart would soon settle down.

"Can I offer you a drink?" Marsh asked. He indicated a small selection of liquor and mixers at the end of the counter. "Or I have beer if you'd prefer."

"I'll have a mixed drink, I think," Pam said. As Marsh had to turn his attention once more to the fish, she added, "I'll fix it myself, since you're busy. Would you like one, too?"

"Thanks," Marsh said. "Whatever you're having will be fine. Scotty, there are some cold soft drinks in the refrigerator. Just help yourself."

By the time Pam had their drinks made, Marsh had finished preparing their dinner. He placed the platter of fish in the warm oven to keep it heated along with the baked potatoes, and then the three of them went out to sit on the porch.

The late afternoon temperature was pleasantly cool as a slight breeze glided landward off the water down the slope. A pair of fishermen edged their aluminum boat to the muddy shore nearest their travel-trailer campsite, ready now to relax at day's end; in the far distance, cars on the Pendleton Bridge skittered purposefully like so many busy ants.

Only half listening to the conversation that ensued between Marsh and Scott concerning baseball and their speculation about who would win the World Series come autumn, Pam found herself gradually relaxing beneath the combined effects of the drink, the cooling air that wafted over her, and the fact that, for the moment at least, absolutely no demands were being made upon her.

"Did you really try to get into the big leagues?" Scotty asked eagerly.

Marsh nodded. "Sure did. But unfortunately I broke my thumb during training camp, so that knocked me out of the running. Since I couldn't play ball that year even if I'd been accepted, I decided to go on to college and work toward my law degree."

"That was tough luck," Scotty said, sincerely disappointed on Marsh's behalf.

Marsh smiled at the boy. "Oh, I don't know. I've been pretty happy with my law practice." He laughed suddenly. "I can see you think there's no comparison."

"Did you get to meet some famous ballplayers?"

Marsh nodded and named a few names that even Pam had heard before. She had to smile herself as she saw how thrilled her son was to meet someone who had been in the company of such illustrious personages. A moment later, while Marsh instructed Scotty on the tricks of throwing a good curveball, she couldn't help but feel herself warming toward him. Scotty didn't often receive such undivided attention from a man, and he was positively reveling in such "man-talk." It forcibly reminded her that her son had no male role model in his young life except Gus, and, before his death, Uncle Bob. As kind and indulgent as those two men had always been to him, they were like grandfathers, not substitute father figures.

The word jolted her when she realized she was thinking of it in connection with this disturbing stranger. Even so, she couldn't quite dismiss it. He was very good with Scotty, and she had never seen her son take to someone so quickly. In a way, she had to be glad for him to find a friend in this man, but in another way it gave her a very uneasy feeling.

"I'm afraid we're boring your mother to tears with all this baseball talk," Marsh said suddenly. He turned to Pam with a warm, apologetic smile.

In spite of her misgivings about him, Pam felt herself responding with a smile of her own. "It's all right," she answered. "I'm hopeless when it comes to sports, and Gus doesn't keep up with the subject too well, either. I'm glad Scotty found a kindred spirit to talk to about it."

"Even so, maybe we should reserve our discussions about it to the times when it's just us men together," Marsh said. "Which reminds me, I was wondering if you'd allow Scotty to go fishing with me tomorrow morning."

"Well . . ." Pam hesitated.

"Please, Mom!" Scotty pleaded, his eyes wide with eager hope.

"Are you sure?" Pam asked, mindful that he was a paying guest, after all, and reluctant to saddle him with an exuberant seven-year-old.

"Sure I'm sure. I'd like his company," Marsh said.

"All right, then," Pam assented, unable to deny Scotty such a rare treat, since normally his fishing activity was restricted to the pier because there was no one available to take him out in a boat.

"Yippee!" Scotty yelped. "Thanks, Mom!"

They went indoors a few minutes later to have dinner. Pam helped Marsh set the table, and the simple meal was delicious. The conversation turned out to be hilarious. Scotty told Marsh about taking a garter snake to school for show-and-tell and how its escape terrorized the teacher and threw the whole class into an uproar. Marsh told of a time when he was nine and played hookey, only to live to regret it once his dad found out and made him do penance by serving as a junior janitor around the school every afternoon for a month. Pam favored them with the story of a time when she and a girlfriend, at age eleven, gave one another home perms with disastrous results.

Once dinner was over, Scotty decided he'd had enough adult company for a while. "Can I go play with those two new boys, Mom?" he asked.

"You mean, the ones staying in the motor home that arrived this afternoon?"

Scotty nodded. "I promised to show them my fort."

"All right. Just be home by dark," Pam told him.

"Be back here by dark," Marsh said, countermanding her orders. "Your mother will still be here."

"Okay." Scotty took off out the door before Pam could object to the new arrangements.

She turned on Marsh at once. "What gives you the right to overrule what I tell my son?" she demanded.

Marsh shrugged, indifferent to her ire. "I wasn't trying to usurp your authority. Since you'll still be here then, it's only logical for him to return here."

"I wasn't planning to stay that long," Pam objected. "I need to get in a little work this evening."

"Nonsense. Didn't your mother teach you it's rude to eat and run? Besides, you need to relax. You're as tightly wound as a clock spring. All work and no play makes Jill a dull girl, you know."

"Maybe so, but this Jill has to make a living for herself and her son, and that's paramount to everything else, including the social graces."

"And who will take care of your son if you have a breakdown from overwork?" Marsh countered. "Surely you can afford to take it easy for one evening. I'll make some coffee."

Pam relented because suddenly it seemed the easiest thing to do. Grudgingly, she admitted to herself he had a point about how rude it would be to leave the moment they'd finished eating. She began clearing the table while Marsh put on the coffee, but he refused to allow her to wash the dishes. He stacked them on the kitchen counter, insisting he would do them later.

When the coffee was ready, they carried it outside. There was a comfortable wooden bench with a high, slat back beneath a tree facing the water, and they sat down on it. For a while they sipped their coffee in companionable silence as the evening slowly descended.

After a while, Marsh stirred. "Gus told me you're alone. It can't be easy, raising a son by yourself."

"No," Pam said quietly, "it isn't." She glanced thoughtfully at him. "I appreciate your kindness to him, and I hope," she went on with a tiny smile, "that you won't regret your invitation to him tomorrow."

Marsh grinned. "No problem. I like kids. I'll enjoy his company. He kind of reminds me of myself at that age, though I'm not sure I ever had such boundless energy."

Pam laughed. "I know what you mean. Sometimes I get tired just watching him. Do you," she asked curiously, "have children of your own?"

Marsh shook his head and, leaning back, stretched his arm along the edge of the bench top. "No, I've not been that fortunate. I was married once, but it didn't last." He gave a slight shrug. "I suppose it's just as well there weren't any children, since it ended in divorce."

"I suppose." Pam gazed somberly toward the water.

"How old was Scotty when your husband died?" Marsh asked.

"Eleven months."

"That's rough." Marsh's voice was sympathetic. "It's a shame he didn't live to see what a fine person his son is growing up to be."

Pam didn't reply. There was no point in telling this man that Mike had never wanted a child, that even had he lived he probably would never have exercised his rights as a father to see Scotty.

As though he sensed that she didn't want to discuss her late husband, Marsh changed the subject. "Do you enjoy living here and running a fishing resort?"

The slight tension she'd felt just thinking about Mike evaporated, and Pam sighed. "It has its pluses and minuses like anything else, I guess. It's a good, healthy environment for Scotty to grow up in, and most of the time I like the slower pace of life here. Of course, summer is our busiest season, but in the winter things slow down a lot and I have more time to myself and for Scotty. Sometimes, though, I miss the kinds of things a city offers . . . libraries, museums, shops, and restaurants. I grew up in Chicago and it was a big adjustment for me when I came here. We're not too far from Natchitoches, and I usually get over there once a month."

"Do you ever get down New Orleans way?"

Pam shook her head. "I've only been there a couple

of times . . . once for Mardi Gras and once to see the King Tut exhibit. Have you lived there all your life?"

Marsh nodded. "Actually, I live in the suburb of Metarie. My father owns an insurance agency there and my mother still teaches school."

"My parents are both gone now," Pam said a little wistfully. "Since my uncle died two years ago, the only family I have left is Scotty. I was an only child and so was my mother. Dad's only brother was Uncle Bob, and he never married."

"It's strange, isn't it," Marsh said softly, "how some people can be so alone while others have swarms of relatives? I've got more kinfolk than I know what to do with—three brothers, their wives, seven nieces and nephews, and so many aunts and uncles and cousins that I can't even keep count."

"You're lucky."

"Think so?" Abruptly, Marsh chuckled. "You might change your mind if you had to buy as many birthday and Christmas gifts every year as I do."

Pam laughed. "I hadn't thought of it that way. Your wallet has my sympathies."

All at once their gazes met and, for a time, neither of them moved. Their laughter faded away and something magical came to possess them, holding them spellbound.

"I like you, Pamela Norris," Marsh said softly.

His words snatched at her breath. Her lips parted and she smiled. "I . . . I like you, too, Marshall Franklin."

Marsh's arm, which had been resting on the back of the bench, suddenly curved around her. His hand pressed against her shoulder, drawing her toward him. His eyes darkened into smouldering hot coals, taking in every inch of her face just before his lips claimed hers.

At first the kiss was light, soft, experimental and infinitely sweet. A rush of intense pleasure filled Pam at the gentle pressure of his lips moving over hers. A moment later he drew away slightly so that he could look at her.

It was a mesmerizing moment. His gaze, soft as a baby's skin, was compelling. A tremor of something, perhaps longing, shook her, and Pam couldn't have looked away even had she been willing.

Those firm lips, gone soft and sensual, fascinated her as his face slowly moved toward hers again.

This time both Marsh's arms were around her and, because there was nowhere else to place her hands, Pam's slid up to encircle his neck as his head bent down and his lips took hers once more.

This kiss was utterly different from the other one. It was demanding, shocking in its intensity. Marsh plundered her mouth, forcing it open, and then he nibbled playfully at her lower lip before his tongue began an erotic probing of the sensitive, inner recesses.

White-hot fire sprang up to lick at Pam's veins. A heady excitement she hadn't experienced for many years came to heighten all her senses. Forgetting everything else, she abandoned herself to the thrill of being pressed to a hard, masculine body, to the warmth of his caressing hands, to the enticing musky scent of him. The fierce thudding of both their hearts commingled into a beat of rising passion.

Marsh's breathing was raspy, her own erratic, when

they finally drew apart. "Pam," he whispered gruffly, "somehow I never expected . . ."

He never got to finish the sentence. From the dark shadows of the camp road came the high-pitched sound of children's voices. Abruptly, Pam pulled away from Marsh's arms, her hands trembling as she reached up to smooth her hair, and a moment later Scotty came into view, bringing along his two newest friends.

Pam was stricken with acute embarrassment over what had just happened and was horrified that she'd actually allowed a virtual stranger such easy familiarities. Although Marsh seemed perfectly at ease and took the sudden appearance of Scotty and the other boys in stride, she was flustered and nervous and could scarcely bring herself to look at him.

Her strange new mood communicated itself to him, and Pam felt Marsh looking at her curiously when she abruptly announced that it was time to go.

"Must you?" Marsh sounded sincerely disappointed. "It's early yet."

"Yes, yes, I must," she said in a rush, avoiding his eyes. "The dinner was lovely, but I do have to go now. Scotty, tell your friends good night. If you're going fishing with Marsh in the morning, you'll need a good night's sleep so you can get up early."

While Scotty was saying good-bye to the other children, Marsh asked in a low, suggestive voice, "And what of you?"

Startled, she lifted her gaze to his face. "What do you mean?"

"Will you be able to get a good night's sleep?" he asked with a teasing gleam in his eyes. "I know for sure

I won't after what just happened . . . especially when I think of all that *didn't* happen!"

Pam felt her face grow warm. "Hush!" she hissed beneath her breath. "Scotty might hear you!"

"So?" Marsh shrugged with unconcern. "He might have seen us kissing, too, but so what? It's not exactly the crime of the century, is it?"

"As far as I'm concerned, it is!" Pam declared. "It shouldn't have happened, and I can't imagine what came over me. Good night, Mr. Franklin," she said stiffly. She turned and began walking away.

"Good night, love," came the soft reply. "Sweet dreams."

Chapter Three

$\mathcal{T}$he morning sky was gray; the sun not yet up. Marsh parked his pickup near the pier and, leaving his gear in back, struck off at an angle toward the store. The only sound in the hush of early morning was the crunching of his boots on the gravel road.

When he reached the store, he rounded the building and climbed the stairs. Just as he lifted his hand to knock, the sun peeped out from behind the trees on the opposite shore, spilling molten gold across the water. It would be a beautiful, clear day.

A moment later, Pam opened the door in answer to his knock. Marsh grinned as his eyes took in her appearance. She wore a pale yellow bathrobe with lace around the edges. The silky cloth fell in soft gathers over her breasts and down to skim her hips. Her hair seemed startlingly dark, and her face, morning-fresh, was clean and devoid of any makeup. Somehow she was at once outrageously sexy and primly modest, and Marsh had to restrain the sudden urge to gather her into his arms and crush all that alluring softness to him.

He successfully managed to keep his hands still, but he could not resist following the powerful impulse to kiss her. Those lovely, naturally pink lips were simply too much temptation to bear. Quickly, he dipped his head and kissed her, enjoying the ripe sweet taste of her.

When he straightened again, he took perverse pleasure in seeing her confusion and embarrassment. Delicate color surged to her cheeks.

"Good morning," he said cheerfully. "Did you sleep well last night? Were your dreams sweet?"

Her blue eyes hardened into chunks of ice. "What I dream," she said in a voice meant to freeze, "is none of your business."

Marsh's eyes twinkled. "Would you like to hear about *my* dream?" he offered. "You were a participant in it."

"I'm not interested in the least," she said repressively. She glanced behind her, as though she were concerned that Scotty might overhear them. With cool politeness, she said, "Scotty's not quite finished with breakfast. Would you like to come inside to wait?"

Marsh stepped into the apartment and glanced around with curious interest. It was a simple place, serviceable rather than showy. Even so, there was a cozy warmth to the room . . . pine paneling and gold-and-rust-colored upholstery. A long shelf on one wall displayed a large collection of books and records; a stand below it housed the stereo; a television set occupied another wall, and opposite it were a recliner chair, a lamp table, and a child's colorful beanbag chair. Near the door was a desk. The room was neat and meticulously clean, mutely testifying to its owner's sense of order.

"Can I offer you some breakfast?" Pam asked.

Marsh's gaze returned to the slender young woman. "No, thanks. But I would take a cup of coffee if you have it."

"Certainly." Pam gracefully crossed the room and went into the kitchen, where Scotty sat at the table. Marsh followed and, making himself at home, sat down opposite the boy.

Scotty put down his spoon, abandoning his half-eaten oatmeal. "I'm ready to go now," he said eagerly.

"Not until you've finished the rest of your breakfast, Tiger," Marsh told him. "You'll need all your strength to haul in all those fish we're going to catch."

Scotty grinned and went back to work on his breakfast. Pam placed Marsh's coffee on the table, then refilled her own cup.

"What time do you expect you'll be back?" she asked Marsh.

"Around noon. I packed a cooler with a couple of sandwiches each and a few soft drinks in case we get hungry, but I imagine by that time we'll be tired and ready to come in."

"I won't," Scotty boasted. "I can stay out all day and not get tired."

Marsh grinned. "Well, I'm not as young as you, pal,

nor in as good shape. By the time the sun starts getting really hot, I'll be wanting to come in and take it easy." He took a sip of his black coffee, then looked up at Pam. "Does Scotty have a life vest that fits him? The only ones I've got are adult-size."

Pam nodded. "We keep it inside the baithouse, and Gus will have it open by now. You can pick it up on the way down."

Scotty drained the last of his milk, wiped his mouth hastily with his napkin, and shoved back his chair. "Come on, Marsh, let's go!" he urged.

Marsh laughed at him. "Can't I even finish my coffee?"

All day long Pam's wayward thoughts kept straying to Marsh during every free moment she had. What was it about the man that threw her off balance so badly? Just the thought of his kisses caused her to tingle and tremble. One would think she'd never been kissed before in her life, much less once been married and even experienced motherhood. She was far too old and mature to have such a severe reaction to a man she didn't even like in the first place!

But that was lying to herself, and she knew it. How could she not like Marsh Franklin? He had a way of taking her by surprise, of doing the unexpected that appealed to some adventurous side of her nature that had long been repressed. He could irritate her to quick, hot anger, then turn right around and be so nice and friendly that she couldn't help but be drawn to him. His smile melted her defenses like the sun beaming down on a snowy field, and she liked the devilish way his eyes could dance and twinkle. He was good to Scotty, which naturally carried its own weight in his favor, and as for his kisses . . .

Her cheeks grew feverish. Pam sternly reminded herself that she should have better sense than to let a man's kisses make her lose all reason. The few other men who had kissed her in all these years since Mike had never had such a devastating effect on her. Not a single one of them had robbed her of a minute's sleep, much less left her shaken and mixed up. She was actually ashamed of herself when she thought of the unduly long time she'd lain awake the night before reliving Marsh's kisses. And this morning, the way he'd pounced on her like a bird of prey, swooping, stealing a kiss before he so much as even said "Good morning"— why must she keep thinking about that?

Fortunately, Pam was quite busy when Marsh and Scotty returned from their excursion. While she was occupied trying to check in two new parties, Marsh poked his head inside the door of the store.

"Just wanted to let you know we're back," he called out. "I sent Scotty upstairs to get cleaned up."

"Fine. Thanks." Pam paused long enough from her work to ask, "Did you have any luck?"

Marsh grinned, and Pam had time to think how animated his face became when he was in a cheerful mood. Somehow his smile blurred the surroundings entirely, so that she was aware of nothing except the magnetism he exhibited, a magnetism, moreover, she was compelled to respond to with matching good humor. The skin crinkled at the corners of his mouth and his gray eyes sparkled like polished silver.

"Pretty good," he answered her, "but I promised Scotty I'd let him have the fun of telling you about it. See you later." With a quick wave of his hand, he was gone.

Over lunch a half hour later, Scotty was full of stories about the fishing trip. He had actually caught one bass himself, and it was, he added proudly, the biggest one of the catch. The fishing was wonderful, the boat was wonderful, the food was wonderful, and, most of all, Pam gathered, Marsh himself was wonderful. Her son's enthusiasm seemed to have no limits.

By the time Pam closed the store and went upstairs around six that evening, however, Scotty's excitement had waned somewhat. The long day had finally caught up with him, and he couldn't stop yawning.

Pam prepared a quick meal of scrambled eggs and hash browns, but Scotty only toyed with his food, too sleepy to take much interest in eating.

Pam smiled at him with fond indulgence and said at last, "If you're not hungry, you can go get ready for bed. You're about to fall asleep in your plate . . . and won't you look silly with egg on your face?"

Scotty grinned weakly and slid from his chair. "It's too early for bed," he objected as a matter of form. "It's not even dark yet."

"I know. Tell you what, get into bed and I'll put the portable TV on your dresser. You can watch it until you're ready to go to sleep."

"Okay." That made the fatigue a little more bearable.

When Pam had him tucked into bed a few minutes later, she said, "I'm going to stretch my legs a bit and walk down to see the ducks, honey. I'll be back in a little while."

Scotty yawned and nodded. He was already interested in the television show, though Pam doubted he'd be able to stay awake long enough to watch it more than a few minutes.

Once she was outside, Pam impulsively headed toward the marina instead of the duck pond. Gus had already gone home, and she wanted to make sure all the aluminum rental boats were securely tied for the night. Yesterday one of their customers had failed to tie up to the pier properly and Gus had spent half the morning searching for the drifting boat.

She found all the boats snugly berthed for the night, but there were several baitbuckets scattered about the pier. Pam gathered them and put them inside the baithouse. After she locked the door, she ambled back onto the pier and sank down on it, crossing her jeaned legs and gazing out over the water.

She was tired this evening, and the cool fresh air revitalized her. Pam tilted her head slightly to get the full benefit of the slight breeze. Sometimes she thought it was ironic that for all she ran a fishing resort for people to come and enjoy the outdoors, she had to spend so much of her own time cooped up inside the store by day, and at night, bent over her desk upstairs in the apartment working on the books.

The vibration of the wooden pier beneath her was her first warning that someone was approaching. Pam half turned to see Marsh coming toward her, and somehow she wasn't at all surprised. Just absurdly glad.

He, too, was wearing jeans, a white western shirt

with sleeves rolled to the elbows, and boots. As though it were the most natural thing in all the world to do, he dropped down beside her, propped up his left leg, and leaned his arm on it. "It was nice out this afternoon, wasn't it?" he asked idly.

"Very. I was just thinking what a shame it is I have to stay inside the store so much every day."

"My thoughts exactly."

"What do you mean?" She half turned her head to look quizzically at him.

"That the store takes up so much of your time. It doesn't leave you a whole lot left for play, does it? And somehow I wish you had more of it."

"Do you now?" The beginning of a smile was forming on her lips. "And why is that?"

Marsh leaned closer to her and practically leered. "So you'd have more time to play with me, of course."

"And what makes you think that's how I'd want to spend my free time?"

Marsh's wicked grin widened. "Because I'm irresistible, of course. Hadn't you noticed?"

"Not at all." Pam stuck her nose in the air. "I can resist you very well, thank you."

"That so?" Marsh's forefinger snaked around her chin and turned her face toward his. "Let's see how well you do." He leaned forward and brushed his lips across hers with the fleeting lightness of a soft breeze. He withdrew just long enough so that he could see the expression on her face and, seemingly satisfied with it, took his time with the next one.

When it ended, he teased, "I didn't notice your doing any resisting."

looked toward Marsh as though he expected him to decently disappear. Marsh gave a good imitation of a wooden Indian. Inwardly, Pam cringed and wondered how to save the situation.

"Marsh is one of our guests, Andy," she elaborated, hoping he, at least, would take the hint to be a little more sociable for the sake of her business. "Today he took Scotty fishing with him."

"How nice for Scotty," Andy said with a grim set to his mouth.

The conversation languished once more. "Er . . . how's your mother's arthritis, Andy?" Pam asked in desperation.

"About the same. Look, I need to be getting along. Walk me back to the truck?" he asked her.

"Let's both walk him back," Marsh suggested silkily. "It's right on the way to my cabin, where I'll make that coffee I promised you, Pam."

Pam glanced at him sharply. Until this moment, there'd been no mention of coffee. That was when she realized Marsh had no intention of leaving her alone with Andy, that the two men had taken each other's measure and she was caught in the middle like a fly in a sticky web. Anger surged in her breast and rose to her throat, nearly choking her. She came close to calling Marsh on his fib. But when she remembered that he was a paying guest and that one in her precarious financial situation did not lightly throw away a lucrative fee like a month's booking, she hesitated. The chewing-out he deserved and would definitely receive would better wait until they were alone.

"All right," she said sweetly. Too sweetly. Marsh

glanced at her with narrowed eyes, not in the least deceived by how well she had swallowed his blatant lie.

Andy appeared clearly unhappy as their trio trod toward his truck. At first he walked slowly, obviously hoping Marsh would go on ahead; when that didn't work, he speeded up, but before Pam could step up her pace to accompany him, Marsh put his arm around her shoulder, leaned heavily against her, and began limping. Pam knew perfectly well the limp was exaggerated for Andy's benefit; it had been only a very slight one that first afternoon when she'd noticed it, and certainly then he hadn't required a crutch, human or otherwise.

When Andy looked back and saw their snail's progress, Marsh graciously apologized. "Sorry about this," he said glibly. "I was in an accident, and my leg still acts up on me sometimes. We'll be along shortly."

Andy grunted and stopped to wait for them. Finally, moving laboriously slowly, they all arrived beside Andy's truck. Marsh leaned against it when Pam abandoned her position beneath his arm.

"I'm glad you stopped by," she said to Andy. "Come again when you can stay longer."

"The real reason I came was to ask if you want to go with me to the club dance this Friday night."

"Well, I . . ."

"What a shame!" Marsh interjected. "She already has a date with me that evening. We're driving into Natchitoches for dinner."

Pam was so startled her mouth almost fell open. She looked toward Marsh, who was smiling blandly at her, but at the sound of Andy's voice she turned once more to him.

"I see," he said in a flat tone of voice. He reached for the door handle. "Maybe another time."

"Y–yes. Umm, I . . . I'm really sorry about that, Andy." Pam searched for some way to soothe him. "We'll definitely plan on the next one. Why don't you come to dinner Thursday night instead?" She darted a warning glance at Marsh. If he came up with "prior" plans for Thursday evening, too, she was certain no jury would hold her responsible if she murdered him on the spot.

But Marsh held his silence this time, and Andy looked somewhat mollified. "That sounds nice," he agreed. "Around seven?"

"That should be fine."

"I'll see you then," Andy said.

He opened the door to the truck, then glanced toward Marsh as he shifted his weight away from the truck bed and stood upright. Barely acknowledging him, Andy slightly inclined his head before getting into the cab. Marsh did the same, his eyes narrow slits as he watched the other man drive away a moment later.

As soon as he was out of earshot, Pam rounded on Marsh. "Just what the hell do you think you're doing, pulling a dirty trick like that?"

Marsh grinned unrepentantly. "It worked, didn't it?"

"And the end justifies the means?"

"Sometimes. In this case, it did. Now, how about that coffee?"

Pam was so furious she was sputtering. "I will not have coffee with you. I'm going home." She turned on her heel and started away.

"Plan to get away early on Friday," Marsh called

after her. "As long as we're going to Natchitoches, I'd like to drop by and visit an old college friend I haven't seen in several years. We'll leave here about two in the afternoon."

Pam wheeled around. "You're crazy!" she exclaimed. "I'm not about to go anywhere with a lying lunatic like you!"

"The next few hours are sure going to seem long if you don't intend to speak to me the whole time."

"Your sneaky, underhanded methods are deplorable," Pam said, breaking her silence as Marsh's pickup turned onto Highway 6.

"Come on," Marsh chided, "did I really do anything so awful? All I want to do is take you off for a while so you can relax and enjoy a nice meal."

"Hmmmph. It's a wonder you don't choke to death on it. Do you always lie so much?"

Marsh flashed her a winsome grin. "Just little white ones. All I did was tell Zelma and Gus you had to do a little shopping and that I was going to drive you to Natchitoches to do it."

"And that afterwards we had plans to go to dinner and might be late getting home. You know good and well I don't have any shopping to do, and you had some nerve asking them to look after Scotty for me."

"I didn't see any signs that they minded. Gus said Scotty spends the night with them quite often when you go out for an evening. Besides, I offered to pick up the wallpaper he has on order there and to exchange that pair of shoes for Zelma, so it works out well for everyone. It frees you for the rest of the day and evening, and we'll be saving them a trip."

Pam sighed. "You're impossible, simply impossible! For a lawyer you sure have a poor sense of right and wrong when it comes to getting your own way."

She had scrupulously avoided him the past two days, ever since Andy had been there, except when she'd been forced to speak to him in the store. Then, out of the blue, Zelma mentioned how glad she was that Pam was going to take a break and go to town with Marsh, and Gus assured her he'd already told Marsh they'd be glad to keep Scotty overnight. Pam had been astounded that Marsh would go behind her back like that, especially when he knew darned good and well she didn't want to go with him.

Yet here she was. Gus and Zelma had both beamed like fond parents because she was going out with such a "nice" man. "He's really taken a shine to you," Gus told her, smiling his approval, "and you could do worse. He's a big-shot lawyer and everything," he'd added, "and besides that, Scotty really likes him, too."

So what did that have to do with anything? Pam wondered irritably. Did Gus and Zelma think that one dinner was going to turn into a marriage proposal? The whole thing was absurd, but because they'd been so glad for her and because Scotty also thought it was great that his mother was going out with his friend Marsh, Pam had held her peace and kept her grave reservations to herself.

"You're not really going to condemn a man for wanting to be with you, now are you?" Marsh asked persuasively. "If you are, then you ought to take those fantastic blue eyes of yours, not to mention"—his eyes flickered briefly over her body before he glanced toward the highway again—"that sensational figure and put yourself in a nunnery. By the way, I really like your dress. White becomes you. It makes your skin look like soft golden silk."

Pam closed her eyes. The man was getting to her again. Her resistance was ebbing. She was, after all, a woman.

Marsh cut his eyes toward her again. He thought—he hoped—that he was winning, after all. What amazed him was why he was so intrigued by this particular woman. Attractive as she was, he'd known more classically beautiful ones. But did any other woman have *quite* such blue eyes? Did any other have such a pleasing profile with that tiny upturned tilt to the nose? He was sure he'd never met another woman who was such an interesting blend of steel and soft vulnerability, of decisiveness and shy confusion, of knowledge yet inexperience. He found himself wanting to know more about her, what made her tick, what things pleased her and what gave that faint, lurking, hurt expression to her eyes during unguarded moments.

"Am I forgiven?" he asked softly.

Pam opened her eyes and smiled at him. "I suppose so," she said grudgingly.

Marsh smiled too and took his hand off the steering wheel for a moment to reach across the seat. He lifted her hand from her lap and gave it a warm squeeze before he released it. "Great," he said. "Now, just look at this gorgeous day. Aren't you glad you came?"

Pam laughed. "Yes. Yes, I believe I am."

On the edge of the small town of Many, they crossed a railroad track and passed a modern discount shopping center and a number of service stations. Like a lot of old towns, the business district along the main street was reminiscent of another era. Weathered brick buildings lined the narrow street, some occupied, some sadly empty, still others in the process of being renovated. The highway itself that wound through town and led to Natchitoches was the historic El Camino Real, the San Antonio Trail on which, if one traveled far enough to the west, would eventually end in Mexico City.

Once they were through the town, they passed green fields where cattle grazed, an occasional home, and forested timberland. To Pam, the drive seemed to go much faster than usual, and she supposed it was because she found herself enjoying Marsh's company. They talked easily about a number of topics, not of great importance in themselves, but which made the time fly.

Almost before she knew it, they had reached the outskirts of Natchitoches and were passing by the sprawling campus of Northwestern State University. It was a fine blend of stately, old red-brick buildings and newer ones that enhanced the dignified atmosphere. The rolling lawns were neat and well manicured.

Marsh glanced at it with interest. "They've added quite a few buildings since the last time I came through here. It looks nice."

Pam nodded. "I think so, too, but I'm a little prejudiced. Northwestern's my alma mater."

"Really? What was your major?"

Pam laughed. "Education."

Marsh grinned. "So naturally, instead of teaching, you took up running a business. Did you ever teach?"

"One year. In Many. But then Uncle Bob's health started to get bad, so I took over most of the day-to-day running of the resort."

"Do you wish you were teaching instead?"

She shrugged. "Not really, though I did enjoy it. After I left Illinois and moved here to live with Uncle Bob, I was determined to go back to school and work for my degree mainly just to have it there to back me up."

While she'd been talking, a strange determined set came to her face. Her eyes glinted and her jaw seemed to tense. There was more, Marsh decided, behind that simple statement that he'd been permitted to glimpse. *Interesting girl,* he thought again.

Natchitoches, which legend said was the Indian word for "Chinquapin eaters," was named after a tribe of Caddo Confederacy Indians said to eat the nut. It had the distinction of being the oldest permanent settlement in the Louisiana Purchase Territory. Founded in 1714 on the Red River, it was at one time a major trading center because of its location. Later, with a change of course by the river, the city was left with only a branch of it, which became the Cane River, and its earlier importance as a dominant trading area lessened.

A few minutes later Marsh turned onto historic Jefferson Street, which meandered along the banks of the Cane River. Here they were immediately plunged into the past. Grand old homes, their brick and cypress beams hand-crafted by slave labor, crowded the narrow street. Pecan and magnolia trees graced lawns and patios. The Prudhomme-Rouquier House, built before the 1800's, was said to be one of the oldest houses in the United States made of *bousillage,* mud.

Abruptly the street became Front Street. Here the pavement was old brick, and along the high bluff which was dotted with commemorative wrought-iron benches and magnolia trees, there was an open view of the placid, flowing river. On the opposite side of the street were the businesses and shops of Ducournau Square. The long wooden structure, trimmed with imported French iron-lace balconies, lent a quaint charm somewhat reminiscent of the French Quarters of New Orleans.

When Marsh parked the car, Pam said, "I think I'll walk down to the river while you visit with your friend."

"What's the matter, afraid we'll bore you silly with 'remember whens?'" His grin was engaging.

"If you're college buddies, I'm sure of it." Pam smiled. "Take your time and don't worry about me. I'll be fine."

She left the bluff and descended the steps to the parking lot. Across from it was the river's edge. It offered a pleasant view of the green slopes beyond, but Pam did not have long to admire it.

Marsh returned in record time. "Gene's out of town."

"It's too bad you've missed him."

He shrugged indifferently. "It doesn't really matter.

His secretary said he'd be back next week. Since it's so near, I'll drive over another day to see him. Well, shall we go get Gus and Zelma's business out of the way? Then we can find someplace to have a drink."

It was after midnight when they climbed the stairs to Pam's apartment laden with packages. Besides the errands they had run for the Emerys, Marsh, overruling Pam's objections, had bought a new baseball mitt, ball, and bat for Scotty, and a box of expensive chocolates and a dozen roses for her. After the shopping, they had enjoyed a marvelous dinner of Natchitoches' famous meat pies and seafood. Later still, they had gone dancing.

Now Pam was pleasantly tired, but it had been such a nice day that she hated to see it end. She deposited her packages on the desk and turned to Marsh with a smile.

"It was fun," she said honestly. "I can't remember the last time I had such a good time."

"I'm glad." Marsh pulled her into his arms and his eyes flickered with unmistakable desire. "I enjoyed it too . . . because I was with you."

His mouth found hers and his hands pressed against her back, molding her pliant form to his. Pam's hands rested on his shoulders before slowly inching upward.

A delicious warmth spread through her midsection and then fanned out in all directions, rendering her weak with an unassauged yearning. His fingers seemed to burn straight through the thin fabric of her dress and her skin tingled where he touched her.

A moment later Marsh pulled her down to the sofa

and the sweet assault of his kisses began anew. Her lips became swollen from the urgency of his mouth on hers before it moved on in search of new, unexplored terrain. A flood of strange desires struck her when his tongue began to tickle her ear, and she quivered when he nibbled at her earlobe.

When his hand came around to cup her breast, Pam stilled, then sucked in a deep breath. Pleasurable sensations sped through her veins, and she only knew that she didn't want such feelings to end. Her own hands slid around his waist and her fingertips dug into his back.

Marsh branded the hollow of her throat with the fire of his kisses. Pam tilted back her head, eyes closed, aching with increasing longing, and when he unzipped her dress and slid it down, she was passive, waiting.

He freed her milk-white breasts from the restraint of the front-hooked bra and then gasped softly. "You're so beautiful," he murmured. He nuzzled her neck and bent lower still to take one throbbing dusky-rose nipple into his mouth.

Pam trembled and laced her fingers through his hair. Her throat tightened and shock waves of desire pounded through her as his ardent lips laid waste to her grip on reality. She inhaled the intoxicating scent of him, thrilled to his lips on her soft flesh and the delight of having his rock-hard masculine body so close to hers. It had been so long that her body was reacting as though it were enjoying a dazzling, brand-new experience. She reveled in each touch, each sensation that built up the tension within her.

She stroked his head and neck. Her fingers moved inside his collar, thrilling to the warm silkiness of his skin.

Suddenly Marsh paused, lifted his head, and, tossing pillows at one end of the sofa, gently pressed her down against them. His smile was soft, passion-filled, as his arms cradled her against him and he kissed her lips once more.

Pam's arms went around him, tugging his shirt from the waistband of his pants. Now her fingers could wander more freely over the broad expanse of his back and around to caress his chest.

Marsh pushed up the skirt of her dress, his hands sliding easily over the curve of her hips. Pam's lower limbs began to ache violently with awakened need. She was fast becoming completely submerged by the insistent demands of her body.

Marsh's own strong needs were apparent, too. The length of his body stretched next to hers was tense with growing passion, and she felt his hard, throbbing masculinity pressed against her.

When he touched the tenderness of her inner thigh, she almost cried out from the pain of wanting. But when he reached up to the waistband of her pantyhose, about to remove them, reality returned, freezing her like a sudden winter blizzard.

What was she doing? she asked herself in sudden panic. Pam pushed against Marsh's solid chest. "No," she gasped. "No, Marsh, we have to stop."

He gathered her to him again, pressing her bare breasts even more firmly to his chest as his lips caressed the corners of her mouth.

"I want you," he whispered huskily. "I want very badly to make love to you, darling." One hand moved down to stroke a breast.

Pam inhaled deeply, trying to ignore the wild sensations his touch evoked, and twisted her head. He made it so difficult to think! "Please, Marsh," she pleaded brokenly. "We can't . . . I can't . . ."

"Why not?" he murmured persuasively. "You want me, too, I can tell. What is it, love? Do you think I might hurt you? I swear I won't . . ."

Pam was close to tears as she finally succeeded in pushing him an inch or so away. "I . . . I'm not worried about that," she choked out. "It isn't that."

Marsh's eyes, dark with passion, now held an expression of confusion and even of faint alarm. "What is it, then?" he asked. "What's wrong?"

She shook her head, unable to explain. How could she possibly tell him that to give in meant opening herself to pain again, allowing a man to have once more the supreme power over her emotional well-being? What if she failed again? She couldn't face it. She absolutely couldn't.

"Nothing's wrong," she said in a low voice. "It's just . . . I just can't make love with you, Marsh. I'm sorry. I should never have allowed things to go this far."

He stiffened. "Is it me?" He sat up abruptly, leaving her exposed and vulnerable. "Did I read all the signs wrong? I thought you cared for me too."

With fumbling fingers, Pam pulled her dress over her shoulders. "I . . . do," she stammered as she struggled to a sitting position, smoothing down the skirt. "But it doesn't necessarily follow that I want to sleep with you, does it? Is that the payment you automatically expect for an evening of dinner and dancing?"

Marsh's face turned a dull red and Pam knew at once that she had gone too far.

"That was crude and uncalled for," Marsh said coolly, "besides being untrue. I think you know that." With a quick movement, he had levered himself off the sofa. "You don't," he added flatly as his cold gaze swept over her, "owe me a damn thing."

Chapter Four

Zelma came into the store carrying a paper bag and set it on the counter Pam was dusting.

"'Morning," Pam greeted from behind the cash register. "What's that?" she asked, indicating the bag.

"Blackberry jam. I made it last night. I brought you some."

"Yummm! Thanks, Zelma. You make the best in all of the South!"

Zelma smiled at the compliment and said modestly, "Maybe not the entire South, but I'll admit my blackberry jam is pretty good." She set two jars on the counter, then picked up the bag to carry to the storeroom. "These other jars are for Marsh."

"Marsh?" Pam was startled. "I've never known you to hand out your goodies to any of our paying guests before."

"We've never had guests who helped Gus and me out before, either, the way he has," Zelma declared.

"What did he do?" Pam asked just before she remembered the errands he'd run for the Emerys the day the two of them had gone to Natchitoches. The day that had ended so disastrously. Just thinking about it brought a lump to her throat.

"He's come over to the house every afternoon this week and helped Gus put up those new kitchen-cabinet doors," Zelma explained. "He even hung my wallpaper for me."

"I had no idea," Pam said quietly. "How . . . how thoughtful of him."

Zelma nodded and confided, "Gus has really been feeling his age lately, and he was dreading the job. I'm not sure he would have been up to doing it alone. Besides that, we've both really taken a liking to Marsh." She chuckled. "He's been so appreciative of the meals I cooked for him, you'd have thought I was doing him a big favor instead of the other way around. You ought to have seen the way he went for my fried chicken last night! There's nothing wrong with that man's appetite! And then he even insisted on helping me wash the dishes after all the work he'd done for us! Can you imagine? You just don't meet many people like him these days."

"No," Pam replied softly, "you sure don't."

She ought not to be so surprised about Marsh's lending a hand to the Emerys like he had, she reflected later, after Zelma had gone to begin cleaning the cabins. A few days ago Pam had seen him helping another guest work on his stalled boat motor, and Scotty told her that when they hadn't been able to get it running again, Marsh had insisted the man go fishing with him in his own boat for the remainder of the man's stay.

As for Scotty himself, he was, Pam thought ruefully, besotted about the man! He had been thrilled over his gifts from Marsh, and several times she had spotted the pair of them playing ball together on the green. As often as he could, Scotty found an excuse to be around Marsh, and, though Marsh never appeared to mind his company, it worried Pam that he must get a little tired of a small child dogging his every footstep. When she'd tried to speak to her son about it, he'd merely given her that sweet puppy-dog look of innocent astonishment and said, "But Mom, he *likes* me!"

Well, Marsh might like her son and he might like Gus and Zelma as well, but it was abundantly clear to Pam that he no longer liked her. For the past week he'd kept his distance from her, and the couple of times they had accidentally met he had been chilly and distant.

She deeply regretted the estrangement between them and was actually amazed at just how much she missed his teasing, friendly attentions. Apparently she had liked him a great deal more than she had realized.

Not that it altered anything. It was too bad that awful night had ever happened, but it had and there was no going back. Somehow Marsh had gotten beneath her wall of defense, something no man since Mike had done, and while she was genuinely sorry she had gotten so carried away and given him the impression she welcomed his lovemaking, she was not at all sorry she had put a stop to things. Still, illogically, whenever she thought of the feelings Marsh had aroused in her, she grew hot and weak and quivery all over again.

The thing that was most terrifying was that those feelings she had experienced with Marsh were far more intense than any her own husband had ever elicited . . . and to Pam that seemed utterly shameful. From the first Mike had found fault with her performance in bed, just the way he'd found fault with practically everything else she did, and now she couldn't help but wonder: if she'd felt such intense passion with him as she had that one night with Marsh, could she possibly have saved her marriage? Unlikely as that was, it was a question that kept gnawing at her.

Even worse, though, was the unshakable conviction that if she had let Marsh make love to her, he would have known her as the failure Mike had known. Just because he had a strange, magical power to excite her didn't mean she could have succeeded in pleasing him any more than she ever had her husband. Even after all these years, Pam wasn't ready to face that particular sort of humiliating defeat again.

She was busy at the desk working on bills when Scotty breezed into the store around eleven-thirty. Pam, glad of a chance to take a breather, tossed down her pen and gave him her full attention.

"What have you been up to all morning?" she asked.

"I helped Gus clean the baithouse."

"Good for you!" Pam praised as he walked around the counter and leaned against her leg. She wrapped her arm around his waist and gave him a hug. "You're an okay kid, you know that?" she asked with a smile. "Maybe I'll just keep you around."

Scotty grinned at the old joke between them. "You're okay yourself sometimes," he returned. "Maybe I'll stick around." Too big for much hugging these days, he inched away from Pam's embrace. "Mom, Marsh wants to know if I can have a picnic lunch with him down by the duck pond. We're gonna eat ham sandwiches."

Pam sighed. *Marsh again.* Everywhere she turned she either saw him, thought of him or heard about him.

"You don't like ham sandwiches," she reminded.

"I do now. Please, can I go?"

"I was going to make your favorite for lunch . . . hotdogs with chili."

"Can't we have that tomorrow?" he pleaded.

"You really want to go on this picnic, hmmm?"

Scotty nodded. "Afterwards, Marsh's going to town to buy some special kind of fishing lures, and he said I could go too."

Pam pursed her lips, but finally she gave a reluctant nod. "All right, but when you get home I want you to straighten up your bedroom. It's a disaster area."

"I will," Scotty promised quickly. He streaked around the counter toward the door, giving her no time for possibly changing her mind. "See you later, Mom. 'Bye."

Thirty minutes later, as she ate her own lonely lunch, Pam couldn't help but feel a slight twinge of envy toward her son. It had been a long time since anyone had invited her on a picnic.

The following morning, Marsh decided not to go fishing that day. He'd had a surfeit of it for awhile. He prepared himself a huge breakfast of sausage, eggs, and canned biscuits which he slathered with Zelma's delicious jam, and ate leisurely as he tried to make up his mind as to how he wanted to spend the day. He could always drive into Many and find some way to kill time there, he supposed. Or, if he was really ambitious, he could drive to Natchitoches to see his friend Gene, and that could kill the entire day. When he'd spoken with him on the phone the day before, after expressing regrets because he'd been away when Marsh had stopped by the week before, Gene had insisted he visit again, saying they'd have a round of golf together and that his wife would love for him to stay overnight with them.

But even the luring bait of a pleasant visit with his old college chum failed to generate Marsh's enthusiasm this morning. Just the thought of Natchitoches brought a sour taste to his mouth because it also brought a reminder of Pam . . . and the way their day and evening there had ended.

He was still as baffled as ever over her inexplicable behavior that night. Not only had they spent a wonderful day and later enjoyed a romantic evening of dinner and dancing together, but after they'd returned to her apartment and he had taken her into his arms, at first she had seemed to welcome his advances.

She'd done more than that, damn her! he seethed. She had invited him to make love to her by the way she had responded to him. She had behaved as though she wanted him every bit as much as he'd wanted her. And boy, how he had wanted her! But then all of a sudden she had stiffened up and turned on the deep freeze, and what he couldn't for the life of him understand was why. She didn't seem at all like the sort of woman who enjoyed teasing a man and then throwing on the brakes just for a cheap laugh.

Marsh shook his head as he got up and began washing his breakfast dishes. Who could figure women? Lynn, his ex-wife, had never liked sex and that had been the primary basis behind the failure of their marriage. After the divorce she had moved back home to live with her parents, and he doubted she would ever marry again. She was too much the little girl. His fiancée, Jackie, had been too much the opposite. She liked all the men a bit too well, and, if he'd married her, it would have been just as disastrous in its own way as his first one had been. But Pam wasn't like either of them. She wasn't a blatant flirt and she sure hadn't acted frigid that night.

Marsh didn't need to be hit over the head with a hammer to make him realize that obviously Pam Norris just plain didn't like him. In a flash she had turned from warm and willing to frosty, and her rejection of him had been cruelly final. He told himself he ought not to care one way or the other, but damn it, he did.

A knock came at the cabin door. Glad to abandon his brooding thoughts, Marsh went to answer it. More than likely it would be Scotty, come to inquire why he hadn't taken his boat out today.

Marsh smiled wryly to himself. His relationship with Pam might not be very cordial, but her son had practically adopted him. It pleased him to think how much that must gall her.

"'Morning, Marsh." It was Zelma Emery, not Scotty. "I came to do up your cabin, but I can come back later. I thought you'd be out on the water by now."

Marsh smiled. "You can come in now. I don't mind. I thought I'd skip fishing today, maybe drive into town for a while. How's Gus this morning?" he asked as he held the door open for her.

Zelma carried the fresh bed linens inside while Marsh took the box of cleaning supplies from her and placed them in the kitchen. "He's not feeling well at all today," she answered. A worried frown creased her brow. "I finally convinced him to stay home and rest, but you know Gus. He's there worrying about all the things that need doing around here."

"Has he seen a doctor?"

Zelma shook her head. "No. But if he's not better tomorrow, I hope I can convince him to go."

Marsh stared thoughtfully at the floor while Zelma went into the bedroom and began stripping the bed. After a moment he followed to the door and asked, "What work did Gus intend to do today?"

Zelma paused to look at him. "Mow the grass, for one thing. Cabin number two has a loose porch step and he was going to fix that, and I think Pam wanted him to check on the wiring in the showerhouse over by the trailer section. There's something wrong with it. Why?"

Marsh grinned. "Well, I'm at loose ends today, so if it'll put Gus's mind at ease, I'll take over his chores. As soon as you get to a phone, call and tell him to stop worrying."

Zelma beamed as though he'd just handed her a fortune. "I will. Thanks, Marsh. Thanks a lot. It's awfully nice of you." A sudden concern crept into her eyes. "But you're not all that well yourself. Your accident . . ."

Marsh brushed aside her anxiety. "I've been improving by leaps and bounds and I'm strong as an ox now. It'll do me good to have a workout. Don't give me another thought." He turned and headed toward the front door.

"But what if Pam objects?" Zelma called from behind him.

Marsh pretended he didn't hear that and kept on going. What Pam thought just didn't matter at all.

He fixed the electrical problem in the bathhouse first; the trouble had been a frayed wire. After that he went to the storage garage where Gus kept the lawn mower, filled the machine with gas, and soon was busy mowing the large center green that divided the camping area from the cabins.

"He's doing what?" Pam asked in astonishment.

"Marsh is mowing the grass," Zelma repeated. "He fixed the wiring in the bathhouse, too. He didn't want Gus worrying about getting so behind." At the strange expression that crossed Pam's face, she asked anxiously, "You don't mind, do you?"

"Mind?" Pam stared at her. "Of course I mind! He's a guest, for heaven's sake!" When she looked at Zelma she saw how upset the older woman was, and she added hastily, "Oh, I'm not angry with you, Zelma. It's not your fault. It's not Gus's either. I'd already decided if he wasn't feeling well by tomorrow I'd call town and see if I couldn't hire someone to come help out for a week or so. But I can't let Marsh do our work!"

"He offered to do it, Pam. Just like when he helped Gus hang our kitchen-cabinet doors."

"That's different. That was at home, a friend helping a friend. This is business!" She went around the counter toward the door. "You watch the store. I'm going to talk to him."

Outside, following the sound of the mower, Pam found Marsh at the foot of the slope behind the store. His back was to her and the blue shirt he wore was perspiration-soaked so that the fabric molded itself around him, emphasizing his broad shoulders and the muscles playing beneath his skin. For one long moment her gaze was riveted by the sight of the blatantly masculine lines of his body, but then she remembered why she had come to find him. Irritation, and yes, even chagrin carried her toward him with long, purposeful strides.

When she drew near, she paused, hands on her hips, as she waited for him to turn the mower around and see her. He finally did and immediately cut the motor. He wiped his moist brow with his arm as she approached and then jumped down to the ground, wincing momentarily as he favored his right leg.

"Whew! Sure is hot today," he observed. He tilted his head toward the sky. "There's not a breeze stirring."

"I didn't come to discuss the weather," Pam said shortly.

Marsh fixed his gaze on her face. "No?" he asked quietly. "What did you come to discuss?"

"You know very well what!" Pam exclaimed. "You can't do this!" Her hand swept outward, indicating the lawn.

Marsh's head turned, his own eyes taking in the short-cropped area where he'd already mowed. "Seems to me I'm doing it without any trouble," he said in a mild tone. "Did you think I was incapable of running a mower?"

"Don't be ridiculous. Of course that wasn't what I meant!"

"What did you mean, then?" Marsh returned his gaze to her, and this time the smoky gray eyes took in more than her face. It flickered over the entire length of her, from her red-and-white-striped knit shirt to her white cotton shorts to her honey-golden legs.

His scrutiny made Pam uncomfortable, and she wished this discussion was taking place with the shelter of the store counter between them. But it wasn't, and there was nothing she could do but endure his meandering gaze.

"I mean you can't do this! You're a guest here, not an employee! I can't allow you to work!"

"I don't recall asking your permission," Marsh said coldly. "I'm doing a favor for Gus. It has nothing to do with you at all."

"Of course it does! I own this place and I say you can't work here."

"What's the matter, think I'll charge too much for my labor? I already told you once, you don't owe me a thing. Not one damn thing."

Pam's face burned from the pointed reminder of that night in her apartment. How could he be so hateful as to bring it up?

She sucked in a ragged breath and tried to stay calm. "Look, let's be reasonable. You're a guest here and you're supposed to be enjoying yourself, not doing other people's work for them. I appreciate your kind intentions on Gus's behalf, but it's really not necessary. If he's out longer than today, I'll hire someone from town to come help out."

"Suit yourself about that," Marsh said, "but I'll still finish what I started today. I'm not expecting your gratitude or a paycheck or anything else, so don't let it worry you." He turned back toward the mower.

"Marsh, please," Pam said urgently. "I wouldn't want any of my guests here to do work, and besides, your leg . . ."

He whirled around again and his eyes were dark and unfriendly. "My leg is fine, so don't waste your pity on me, lady."

Pam's throat felt scalded with sudden tears. Marsh disliked her so much now that he couldn't even tolerate any genuine concern on her part. She held out a hand in an unconsciously pleading gesture. "Marsh," she began huskily, "I know we . . . the other night . . . I'm sorry . . ." She wasn't being coherent at all and, realizing it, she broke off, her eyes eloquently speaking what her voice couldn't say.

"Forget it," Marsh said curtly. "It's a closed episode as far as I'm concerned, and I have no intentions of rehashing it." His gaze swept beyond her shoulder and his jaw clinched. In a low voice, he added, "You have company."

Pam turned to see Andy approaching them. Why, she wondered, disheartened, did he always have to show up when Marsh was there?

If her greeting lacked a certain something as far as enthusiasm went, Andy didn't seem to notice. His eyes were on Marsh, the way one might warily watch a strange dog.

Marsh, however, couldn't have been more cordial. It seemed to Pam he was quite pleased to see the other man. You'd have thought they were best friends the way Marsh smiled and extended his hand. "Nice to see you, Graham," he said heartily. "Is this weather hot enough to suit you?"

Andy looked a bit taken aback, but he quickly regained his composure. He shook hands with Marsh and managed a smile. "Good to see you again. How's the fishing been?"

For the next few minutes the two men exchanged stories about their respective fishing trips while Pam stood to the side wondering what to make of it all.

Finally, Andy turned toward her. "I came to invite you to come to my sister's birthday party tonight. Her husband's throwing a barbecue and having a few friends over and I thought maybe you could come with me."

"Thanks, Andy, but I can't tonight," Pam said. "Gus is sick today, so I can't possibly ask Zelma to keep Scotty for me."

"That's no problem," Marsh said suddenly. "I'd be happy to stay with him this evening while you're out."

Pam stared at him as though he'd lost his mind. She couldn't believe her ears. He looked back at her with a bland, guileless expression as though there wasn't anything in the least unusual about his offer.

"Hey, that'll be terrific!" Andy said quickly. "That's awfully decent of you, Franklin." He turned back to Pam. "I'll pick you up around six."

She shook her head. "Oh, no, I don't think I—"

"Sure, you can," Marsh said. "You need to get away and relax. You just go on with Graham and have a good time and don't worry about a thing. You know as well as I do that Scotty'll be perfectly content with me for a few hours."

Pam couldn't argue with that, but she could argue about the fitness of the whole situation. It seemed to have been taken out of her hands. Before she could come up with a real argument against the plan, Andy said a quick good-bye and was gone, and Marsh, without another word, climbed back on the mower, started it, and rode away from her.

The evening was a disaster from start to finish. Pam felt like a fool when Marsh arrived to stay with Scotty and behaved like a benevolent older brother toward her. His gaze was entirely impersonal as he took in her appearance, from her beige slacks to the gold-colored blouse. He assured her that Scotty would be just fine in his care and that he would enjoy an evening of video games. When Andy came for her, he cheerfully told them to have a good time, but reminded Andy not to keep her out too late since she had to work in the morning. It all irritated Pam to no end. She didn't want Marsh Franklin for a brother. Not even a kindly one!

She also knew she didn't want Andy for anything more than a friend, and that created more problems. At the party, for some reason she didn't understand, his family, all of whom she'd met numerous times before, treated her as a part of them, while Andy hovered at her side, almost suffocating her with solicitous attentions she'd never been aware of his doing on their previous dates. It all smacked of serious intentions, making Pam acutely uncomfortable.

When they returned to the resort late that night and Andy parked his car, he turned to her in the darkness and, pulling her into his arms, said huskily, "You know I'm crazy about you. Don't you think it's time we thought about making plans for the future?"

Pam was dismayed. Gently she disentangled herself from his arms, and her voice shook when she spoke. "Andy, no. Please don't say anything more. I really like you a lot and I've enjoyed going out with you, but that's all."

"That's all?" Hurt coated Andy's voice. "But I thought we were heading toward something serious . . . toward marriage. I want to marry you, Pam."

"I'm sorry." There was a catch in her throat. "I'm really sorry, but I can't. I don't feel that way about you, and to tell the truth, I'm not sure you really feel that way about me. I think you've just decided it's time for you to get married, but we've never been really serious about each other. I'm not," she added softly, "the right woman for you."

"How do you know for sure?" he asked. "Maybe we haven't had that intense of a relationship, but we get along so well and I'd be good to you. And to Scotty," he added as an afterthought.

Pam smiled wryly, glad he couldn't see her face in the dark. Among all the other reasons why marriage with Andy would be wrong, his afterthought about Scotty was a very important one. If she ever did remarry, which was only the most remote possibility, the man would have to truly care about her son as well as herself, not just consider him excess baggage.

"It just wouldn't work," she said with quiet finality.

Andy sighed. "Is there any chance you might change your mind in the future?" he asked.

Pam shook her head. "I'm afraid not. To be honest, Andy, I'm not sure I'm the marrying kind. I value my independence too much."

"Will I see you again?"

"It would only be a waste of your time," she said gently. "Look around for someone else, and forget about me. You deserve the best and I know she's out there somewhere." Before he could continue the pointless discussion any further, she opened her car door and got out. "Goodbye. You're a great person, Andy. Good luck."

Pam hurried toward the stairs beside the store, but

she didn't mount them until Andy drove away. She was sorry she'd had to disappoint him, but she knew what she'd done was right for them both. Slowly she mounted the steps.

When she entered the living room, she saw Marsh at once by the dim lamplight. He was sprawled on the sofa, arms crossed, eyes closed and his soft, regular breathing told her he was asleep. Something about seeing him that way affected her strongly. It seemed so intimate, so private, so touching. Something softened inside of her and it was some minutes before she could draw her gaze away from him.

Pam dropped her purse to the coffee table and slipped off her shoes. Then she went quietly through the hall to Scotty's room, where she found her son also asleep. She brushed a lock of hair away from his forehead and bent to kiss it before she tiptoed out again.

When she returned to the living room, she hesitated uncertainly. Marsh looked so peaceful she hated to wake him. There was a pleasant, unguarded look to his face and his lips were curved into a slight smile, as though he were enjoying his dream. It seemed a shame to wake him, but on the other hand, she could scarcely allow him to sleep here all night.

At last she went to him and lightly shook his shoulder. "Marsh?" she said softly, trying not to startle him. "Marsh, I'm back, and you can go now. Wake up."

"Hmmmm, nice," he mumbled. "Nice." His arm went out and his hand closed around Pam's arm. He pulled her closer, then down as his other arm went around her waist. Pam found herself suddenly pressed to his chest while his lips moved warm and caressingly on her neck. "My soft love," he whispered. "Love."

Pam went hot with embarrassment. He was dreaming about someone and he thought she was that woman. She needed to wake him up fast, but at the same time her senses were coming vibrantly alive as Marsh's hands stroked her back and his mouth traveled upward to her chin, her cheeks, and finally found her lips.

She stiffened, resisting him for an instant. She couldn't allow this to happen. But when a warm rush of ecstasy raced through her as his lips moved over hers, Pam weakened and forgot herself as the clamoring responses of her body took over.

Marsh's hands went down to press against her hips, fitting her contours more closely to his while his mouth continued to possess hers, stimulating her to new, exalting heights.

Pam allowed herself the daring indulgence of touching his face, stroking his cheek with the gentleness of a butterfly's wings. But when one of his hands took the fullness of her breast within it, her response grew more intense and she quivered, surrendering totally to the sensual emotions he aroused. Her hand raked through his hair, then down to cling to his shoulder.

Marsh was no longer asleep. His slumberous eyes met hers as he put both his hands between them and began to open her blouse. Pam already was too far gone to stop him even if she'd wanted, only this time she knew she didn't. Right or wrong, she wanted the fulfillment that her body was demanding. She wanted only to feel, to experience, and, following that instinctive desire, her hands roamed downward to tug his shirt free of his pants.

As his hand slid inside her bra to touch the soft silkiness of her skin, Marsh asked, "How was your date with Andy?"

Pam shrugged. She didn't want to talk about that . . . or even to think about it. She wanted only this moment, this man, and the wondrous sensations that she was feeling. "So-so," she said dismissingly. Marsh's fingertips were wreaking havoc on her as they traced her nipple, causing it to thrust upward into a hard peak. She bent forward to plant a kiss at his throat and then began to unbutton his shirt.

"You're not interested in him, are you?" he asked.

"Who?" she asked vaguely. Her entire attention was on the intoxicating male scent of him as she nuzzled his neck and began to nibble at his earlobe.

"Graham."

Pam paused while her fingers continued their foray through the soft dark forest of fur on his chest. "No," she whispered huskily. "I'm not interested in him."

"I knew that," he said with satisfaction. "That's why I offered to stay with Scotty while you went out with him. I could tell you didn't want to go."

"So you did it just to annoy me?"

Marsh nodded before kissing her bared shoulder. "And what is it you do want?" the soft voice asked. "Do you want me?"

Pam closed her eyes. Must he make her say it out loud? Her throat squeezed shut. "I . . . I . . ."

"Say it," Marsh ordered thickly. "Say it, Pam. Tell me you want me to make love to you."

Pam sucked in a sharp breath. Marsh was paying her back for that other night. Because she hadn't been able to go through with it then, he'd been furious, and now he was deliberately making the moment as awkward for her as he could. Warring emotions fought within her. Her whole body was on fire, aching for him, needing release, but she couldn't admit it in words. It was cruel of him to try to make her do it.

"I . . . I can't," she whispered at last. Her voice cracked over the words.

She felt Marsh's entire body stiffen. "I see." He shifted their position so quickly she scarcely knew what was happening. All at once she lay on the sofa alone while he towered above her, rebuttoning his shirt while the dark coals of his eyes blazed scornfully.

"Just what is your game?" he asked harshly. "You've already rejected me once. Now you come in here again acting all cuddly and steamed up, but you won't admit you want me. Were you about to throw a clinker in the works again just for kicks?" Without giving her time to reply, he grated, "I'll save you the trouble this time. I don't enjoy playing the fool."

Chapter Five

I mean it," Gene Douglas said. He squinted at Marsh through a blue haze of cigarette smoke. "Since Dad died last fall, I've been on the lookout for a new law partner, and you'd be perfect. We'd make a great team. Give it some serious thought, will you?"

They were in a small bar near Gene's office. At two o'clock in the afternoon they had the place to themselves while they caught up on news.

Marsh tapped his fingertips on the laminated tabletop, then lifted his glass of Scotch to his lips. The dark amber liquid burned his throat as he swallowed. "I don't know, Gene," he replied. His eyes darkened thoughtfully. "To tell the truth, I've been thinking along the lines of setting up practice either here or in Many and buying myself a place on the lake. I like it there. The pace is so relaxing and that appeals to me. On the other hand, you just don't lightly toss away an already established practice." He shrugged his massive shoulders. "My recovery from the accident has forced me to slow down a lot for the time being, but I can't help wondering if I'd really hate it in the long run if I did make such a move. My family's in New Orleans, you know, and I'm not sure whether I want to move across the state from them."

"It's a lot to consider," Gene conceded. "I'd really like working with you if you want to come in with me, but there's no hurry about making up your mind. Take all the time you want."

"Thanks, Gene." Marsh grinned. "It is a tempting offer."

"So . . ." Gene's tone changed to a light, teasing one, "now that we've got that out of the way, tell me why you aren't married with three kids, a wife, a dog, and a mortgage hanging around your neck like the rest of us from the old gang?"

Marsh laughed. "Put like that, it sounds as though I've had a lucky escape. You knew of course that my marriage to Lynn went down the drain." At Gene's nod, he went on quietly, "I was engaged again, but that ended a few months back. Unfortunately"—he gave a slight shrug—"that was a mistake, too."

"Dick Palmer called me after your accident," Gene admitted. "He said your fiancée was driving the car the night you were injured. Was she hurt, too?"

"Only a couple of bruises and scratches, thank God," Marsh said with unmistakable sincerity. "I'm really glad she wasn't hurt, and I don't resent her for what happened to me. She was genuinely sorry about it."

"But the engagement was still over?" Gene asked quietly.

Marsh inclined his dark head. "I'm still fond of her, but I had a lot of time to think in that hospital bed, and I realized marriage for us would never have worked."

Marsh and Jackie had been to a party the night of the accident and taken Jackie's car because Marsh's had been in the repair shop. She drank a bit too much and hung all over a politician, and when they got back in the car, they got into a heated argument about her behavior.

Jackie had refused to let Marsh take the wheel, and she'd shot the car down the street like a cannonball. They had both been furious, and Marsh had said some pretty nasty things to her. So in a way, he couldn't blame her entirely for the accident. After all, he'd done a lot to provoke her.

Later, while he'd been stuck in the hospital bed with plenty of time to think, he'd really analyzed their relationship. While he could forgive Jackie for the accident and his injuries, he came to realize he simply didn't want the same things out of life that she did. She loved to party and mingle with what she called the "right" people—rich, important people. Jackie had never wasted time on anyone she didn't think could somehow be beneficial in her life, and Marsh just couldn't base his own friendships on the size of someone's wallet or their political or social clout. He was wealthy himself through a number of good investments he'd made, but he'd never thought it in any way made him above anyone with less money than he had.

But the main reason he'd broken the engagement wasn't Jackie's social-climbing aspirations, but her easy, flirtatious ways. Marsh couldn't see himself worrying and wondering the rest of his life whether she'd cheated on him every time he saw her get too friendly with other men. That just wasn't the way he wanted to live.

Marsh polished off his drink and motioned to the waitress to bring another. "Your turn. Tell me about the kids, the wife, the dog, and the mortgage."

Gene laughed and proceeded to do so. Contrary to the negative ring of his earlier comment about the subject, as he displayed pictures from his wallet of his family and spoke with pride about his wife's work as a speech therapist and his children's achievements in school, Marsh felt a stab of pure envy. It all sounded so normal, so nice, so . . . so purposeful.

The problem was that at thirty-five, Marsh had had more than enough of a bachelor's existence. He was successful in his practice as well as fortunate with his investments, but money and success just weren't enough anymore. Sometimes he had the feeling his life was slipping by without having any firm direction, without any real point to his existence at all. He lived in a luxurious condominium, traveled whenever and wherever he chose, and could afford to buy just about anything he desired, but he knew in his heart that his brothers and friends like Gene were the lucky ones in spite of mortgages and orthodontist bills. They had roots, wives and children to give their lives stability and a meaning that his lacked.

A vision of Pam came to mind. Somehow Marsh had a gut-level instinct that she could make a fine wife, the way Gene's wife sounded. Beautiful in a refreshingly honest way, there was caring and compassion in her. The sun obviously rose and set on her son, giving her a maternal tenderness that brought a lump to Marsh's throat just thinking about it. She was a busy, hard-working, modern young woman, running a business. And yet there was nothing of a brittle hardness about her. Anyone could see that she genuinely loved Gus and Zelma, and that they returned that love. Conspicuously absent in their relationship was the normal strain and tension in an employer–employee situation. It simply didn't exist.

He must be mad to even think of Pamela Norris in the context of a wife, Marsh thought a half hour later as he left the outskirts of Natchitoches and headed back toward the resort. Like him, she had a failed marriage behind her. For a topper, the two of them didn't even get along! How clear did she have to make it to him that she simply wasn't interested?

Marsh shook his head. He didn't understand either of them. Why did Pam continually behave as though she wanted him, and then, at a crisis point, bring things to an ignoble halt? And why did he even care? Why did he stick around? What kind of man liked to be kicked in the teeth over and over?

God knew he'd had enough of that sort of thing in his marriage. How many times had Lynn pretended to be asleep when he came to bed, or else had the classic headache? Yet he'd stuck it out for three long years, hoping it would get better, hoping that if only he were patient she would lose that tenseness of hers. She never had.

But Pam wasn't like Lynn, not really. There was something warm and giving about Pam that Lynn had lacked entirely. The way she accepted his kisses, returned his caresses, told him that. But in the end, she kept freezing up. She wanted him, yet she didn't want him. The whole thing was crazy and inexplicable. If he had any sense, he'd pack his bags and leave the resort this very afternoon. There was nothing to keep him, so why didn't he just go?

Well, maybe not *this* afternoon, he decided as the first huge raindrops spattered on the hood of the pickup truck. All day the gray skies had been threatening rain; now the threat was made good as the large drops fell hard and heavy. Marsh sighed gloomily, decreased his speed, and switched on the windshield wipers. Ahead of him were several loaded logging trucks he'd just been about to pass. Now, with the downpour, he didn't dare try, and he was frustrated and impatient at the holdup. Not that there was anything to hurry back to when he did reach the resort, he reminded himself sourly.

"Are you sure you don't want us to stay?" Zelma asked.

"I'm sure," Pam said firmly. "In this downpour I don't see us selling bait or renting any boats this afternoon. You both may as well take advantage of the weather and enjoy the rest of the afternoon at home.

Besides, if the rain gets any worse, you might have a hard time getting home. Now, shoo! Gus is waiting for you in the car."

"All right, if you're sure," Zelma said. "See you in the morning."

Pam crossed to the window and looked out at the driving rain as Zelma made a hasty dash toward the car. A moment later it was gone, and Pam felt an odd loneliness steal over her.

It was silly to feel that way, of course. Just because Scotty was in town staying overnight at his friend Jimmy's house and now Zelma and Gus were gone, there was no reason to feel abandoned and alone. After all, she had told them to go, and besides, the resort was filled to capacity at the moment. She wasn't truly alone.

She was gratified that business was picking up. Today she'd got several new bookings for the latter part of the month and on into July. Even so, if she were to have one hundred percent occupancy for the rest of the summer, it would still be shaving things close. *Those darn loans,* she thought in despair. If only those debts didn't exist.

Pam's shoulders drooped as she peered through the window at the dark gray shroud of rain. The marina across the road was only an indistinct blur.

Sometimes she got so desperately tired of juggling bills, paying a little here one month and a lot there, then vice versa next time around. Even when something got paid off there was scant satisfaction in it because by that time something else had broken down and she had a new bill to take its place.

Maybe it was just all too much for her. Uncle Bob

could have been wrong in his faith in her to carry on this place he had established. Mike had probably been right once when he had told her business procedures were simply over her head and that he wasn't about to waste his time trying to explain such things to her.

She laughed grimly. The harsh sound was eerie in the silent store. If Mike were alive today he would be astounded to know she'd managed to hang on to a business this long. But then Mike had never believed she could do anything, including run a household without his advice and interference. And somehow, *somehow* she would manage to hang on even longer, just to prove him wrong, even though he would never know. But she would know and that was the important thing. Her self-confidence and self-respect were at stake. If she just threw up her hands and quit, like she sometimes felt like doing, she would only be reinforcing what he had thought of her all along.

A truck came into view beneath the gray blanket of rain. Marsh's truck. Pam recognized it immediately. It slowly passed the store and a moment later was lost to sight as it rounded the bend and vanished behind the towering pines.

Pam closed her eyes as a great wave of intense regret overcame her. Never had she desired a man so much as she had Marsh last night, and yet, cowardly, she had been unable to ask for what she wanted. Even now she cringed at the thought of putting into words her most secret yearnings.

Yet her inability to do so had alienated him. Because of her withdrawal that first night, Marsh had demanded that she verbally express her wishes last night, and she couldn't altogether blame him for that. A man's ego and sensitivity could be so easily bruised, and obviously he had been hurt that first time. But she just couldn't say it, even for him.

Even for him. Why had she thought of it in quite those words? As though Marsh were truly important to her, more so than any other man. Yet it was only the truth. He *was* important to her, and the thought was frightening. Somehow it represented a threat to all she had worked toward for so long, all she had become.

But what was it about Marsh that made him out of the ordinary? He had rugged good looks and the physique of an Olympic athlete. He was unquestionably the kind of man that caused women to look twice, but that didn't explain the devastating assault he could make on her senses just by a mere glance. She had known other good-looking men and never so much as felt a flutter. Yet Marsh had only to look at her and her bones melted; his slightest touch instantly changed her blood to a fiery fluid that burned its way through her veins. With Mike, in the beginning at least, she'd felt a mildly pleasant warmth. But a raging inferno? Never! Until Marsh, she hadn't believed such reactions were real. She'd thought they were only an invention of romance novelists and movie-makers.

So what did it all mean? Obviously there was some sort of strong physical chemistry between her and Marsh, but did it have any meaning beyond sexual attraction?

The answer escaped her, and Pam sighed. She didn't want to think about the matter anymore. In fact, she didn't want to think about Marsh at all. It only confused her and brought a strange, heavy pain to her heart.

She turned back to the counter and began rearranging the conglomeration of impulse-sale items there. She picked up a cardboard stand with cigarette lighters and swapped it with a display of postcards. When this little chore did nothing at all to enhance the looks of the counter, she realized in frustration that she was merely creating busywork for herself exactly the way a schoolteacher will assign such a task to a class of unruly first-graders at the end of a long day.

By a quarter to five, the rain was still falling, though not quite so violently as before. The sky was dark gray, as though an early nightfall was approaching. Deciding that a few minutes one way or the other wasn't going to make much difference on a day like this, Pam closed the store early. Since Scotty was away overnight, she had the unexpected luxury of a free evening ahead of her, and she would take full advantage of it. There would be no work tonight on such things as bringing the books up to date or paying bills or doing laundry or other small chores around the apartment. Instead, she would pamper herself the way she so rarely had time to do. She would take a long soaking bath with scented bath oils and a paperback novel she'd bought over a month ago and never had time to read. She would shampoo her hair and polish her nails. Then, in her nightgown and robe, she would make herself a BLT, pour a glass of milk, and have her supper in front of the television.

Suddenly, through the sound of pounding rain came another sound. Pam had just been about to step off the porch and race toward the stairs, but the sound caused her to pause, listening. It had sounded like children's voices.

It came again, and this time she realized it came from the direction of the marina. While it was distant and she couldn't understand the words, the high-pitched, panicked sound sent ice water pumping through her veins.

Even as she jumped off the steps and began running toward the marina, she heard the voices for a third time, and now she knew for certain it *was* children's voices and the children were in trouble!

Pam's heart lodged in her throat as she ran across the road. "Hold on!" she shouted at the top of her lungs. "I'm coming!"

She was panting, as much from terror as from exertion, when she reached the marina. She was aware of an ominous silence except for the pelting rain. It was as though nothing, nothing were alive except for the storm. "Please God," she prayed raggedly as she raced around the baithouse and past it toward the pier.

She saw them the moment her feet pounded onto the wooden pier. One of the aluminum rental boats had broken free of the mooring, and now it bobbed aimlessly in the water, a good quarter of a mile from shore. Inside it she could see two small forms, one seated, one standing; her heart lurched when she realized neither of them wore the telltale bright orange of a life preserver!

She cupped her wet hands around her mouth and shouted, "I'm coming! Sit down! I'm coming to get you!"

She couldn't tell whether the children heard her. It wasn't likely that they had. The wind was blowing in her direction, snatching her words and carrying them behind her. Pam ran to another of the rental boats, praying there was gas in the tank as she bent toward the rope that secured it to the piling.

A strong hand suddenly touched her arm and a voice, raised above the storm, said, "Let's take my boat. It's got a full tank and it's faster."

Pam looked up to see Marsh beside her and was suddenly relieved that she was no longer alone. His face was grave, wordlessly telling her he, too, understood the extreme danger of the situation. With a jerk of her head, Pam nodded and, when he moved swiftly away, followed him down the pier to his boat.

Marsh wasted no time aiding her into the boat. He jumped into it first and switched on the engine. Pam stopped on the pier long enough to untie the rope and, still holding the end of it, jumped into the boat just as it began to inch away from the pier.

The rain lashed their faces, almost blinding them, as they picked up speed and bounced across the rough waves. Pam rubbed her eyes, clearing them of moisture, and strained to see the silvery boat ahead of them. Sky and water were an angry gray and full darkness was only minutes away. Already it was growing more and more difficult to see through the heavy gray sheet of rain.

The children finally saw them. Pam waved and they waved back. Then her heart lodged in her throat when the second child jumped to her feet and the aluminum flat listed precariously.

The children grabbed on to the edges of the boat and sank to their knees; Pam muttered a prayer of thanks.

If only they would remain still until she and Marsh could reach them, they would be safe.

Reading her mind, Marsh stole a brief glance at her. "They'll be all right," he shouted encouragingly above the roar of the rain. "We'll soon have them safe."

Two minutes later they drew near the other boat. Marsh cut the speed, then pulled up horizontally beside it. The two children, whom Pam now recognized as the young son and daughter of a couple named Hill who had arrived at the resort the previous day, crouched in the bottom of the boat, crying and shivering and wide-eyed with fear.

"You hold us steady," Marsh instructed Pam. "I'll get them." He found the rope that dangled from the bow of the aluminum flat and tossed it to her. Pam tugged at it with all her strength until she brought the two boats side by side. Marsh leaped into the children's boat while she held it steady.

The transfer of the children from one boat to another was accomplished without mishap, although they were both sobbing uncontrollably as Marsh handed them one by one to Pam's waiting arms. When they were both with her, he stepped back in, took the rope from Pam, and tied the aluminum boat to his so that it would float alongside as they made their way back to shore.

The trip back was slow because of the burden of the aluminum boat and Marsh's concern that it might damage his own. Pam's hands were filled with the children as she cuddled them in her arms and crooned soothing words to them.

"What made you get into the boat in the first place?" she asked after they had calmed a bit.

"We thought it would be fun to go for a ride," the little boy told her.

"In the rain?"

"It wasn't raining so hard when we went," the girl said.

"Where were your parents?"

"They were taking a nap," the boy said. "We were tired of playing in the cabin and waiting for them to wake up."

Pam shivered at what a close call they'd had. "You must promise never to get into a boat again without an adult with you, and even then you must wear life jackets."

"We w-w-won't," the little girl stammered over her hiccups. "It was so s-c-cary when the rain came harder and the boat was rocking."

"Aw, I wasn't scared," the boy boasted. Pam fixed him with a stern glare, and he backed down. "Well, maybe just a little. We won't do it again."

Pam hugged him to her. "I know you won't," she said gently.

When they reached the dock, a small cluster of people were waiting there. In addition to the children's parents were several other guests at the resort whom the parents had enlisted to aid in the search for the children once they'd realized they were missing.

When it was ascertained that the children were no worse the wear because of their adventure, the others soon scattered, eager to get out of the rain, while the parents thanked Marsh and Pam profusely. It continued for an embarrassingly long time and Pam finally ended it the only way she knew how, by pointing out that the children were wet, cold, tired, and probably hungry and should be carried back to their cabin. At last the family went away, and Pam and Marsh were left alone on the pier.

They looked at each other and burst out laughing as relief overtook them both. Marsh's smile was incredibly tender as he took in her wet, bedraggled appearance, and Pam caught her breath as he reached out to push the sodden hair away from her face. "You're dripping," he said. A teasing light flickered in his eyes as he gazed down at her.

Pam smiled. "So are you." She rather liked the look of him all wet. His hair was dark and sleek, his skin glistened, and his clothes molded to his frame, starkly outlining the power of his muscles. Suddenly she shivered, becoming aware that not only were they both wet, but it was growing quite chilly as well. "Maybe we'd better get out of the rain," she suggested. "Can I . . . can I offer you some coffee?" Remembering the last time they'd been together, she realized her invitation was bold and daring, that he might cut her dead, and once the words were out, she tensed, waiting for his answer.

Marsh's gaze was piercing, as though he could read what was really behind the question. After a moment, he nodded. "I'd like that," he said slowly. "I'll change into some dry clothes first and then I'll join you."

When she reached her apartment, Pam put on the coffee, then hurriedly stripped away her soggy clothes before stepping beneath a hot shower. A few minutes later, as she dried off with a thick towel, she heard a knock at the door.

Marsh already. Quickly, she threw on her robe and went toward the door.

One hand fluffed her still damp hair as Marsh entered the living room, dressed now in dry Levis and a beige shirt. He shrugged out of a moisture-beaded red windbreaker and hung it on the coatrack by the door. "It's raining harder than ever," he told her. "Thank God we found those kids before it got dark. We'd have a devil of a time out looking for them now."

"I thought of that, too. It gives me the shivers." Marsh turned to give her his full attention, and at once Pam felt self-conscious and awkward. "The coffee should be about ready," she told him hastily. "Just help yourself while I get dressed."

"You're dressed all right as far as I'm concerned," Marsh said, surveying her with an impersonal eye. "You look comfortable and warm and you're quite modestly covered up, if that's what's worrying you. You don't need to change on my account. Just lead me to the coffee."

After that little speech and the total lack of interest in his expression, Pam felt she would seem ridiculous if she insisted upon changing, so she tried to forget the fact that she was naked beneath the heavy folds of the robe as she turned toward the kitchen.

"There's some brandy in the top cupboard to your left if you'd like some in your coffee," she said as he followed her to the kitchen and watched while she poured the scalding dark liquid into two cups.

"Just what we need to warm us up after the soaking we've had," Marsh said approvingly. He found the brandy and liberally laced both cups with it.

Pam carried the tray into the living room and placed it on the coffee table. Marsh sank into an easy chair while she sat down on the sofa, and she breathed a little easier with the safe distance between them. Already, just having him here in her home, there was an entirely different feeling to the atmosphere, a vibrant, unleashed energy, intangible, yet no less real because it was unseen. It was as though Marsh completely dominated the room; certainly, he dominated her awareness.

Marsh seemed oblivious to the nervous tension that had come over her. He leaned back in the chair, took a sip of his coffee, then asked curiously, "Where's Scotty?"

"In town staying overnight with his friend, Jimmy." Pam's lips curved into a wry smile. "The silence without him is deafening, isn't it?"

Marsh chuckled. "I suppose that's the way it is with all kids. They don't let you forget they're around for a minute, do they?"

"That's the truth," Pam sighed. She paused, then went on softly, "I have to thank you for all the attention you've paid him. He thinks you're the greatest thing that's come along since Santa Claus."

Marsh grinned. "I kind of like him, too. He's been a lot of company to me since I've been here."

Pam nodded. "And vice versa. I hate to think how much he's going to miss you when you leave."

"Maybe I can still see him from time to time," Marsh surprised himself by saying. "I could come back on occasional weekends; perhaps sometimes you'll let him spend a few days with me in New Orleans."

Pam looked startled. "Why would you want to do that?" she asked incredulously. "He's just a little boy, after all!"

Marsh shrugged and narrowed his eyes in thought before he replied. "He's exactly the kind of son I'd like to have myself," he said honestly. "He's a tough little kid and smart as a whip besides having a terrific personality. He could," he added with a soft smile, "easily hold his own with my slew of nephews and nieces."

Pam laughed and could almost picture Scotty in the midst of Marsh's large family as he described them to her. It sounded wonderful, their family get-togethers with his parents, brothers, their wives and children. It must be so lively and fun. She had always envied large families and regretted that she was an only child, just as she felt an occasional twinge of sadness because Scotty not only had no brothers or sisters, but no father or grandparents either.

After a while, Pam got up and heated a stew she had made the previous night. Throughout the simple meal, Marsh kept her entertained with tales of the numerous hijinks he and his brothers had pulled throughout their growing-up years.

They had just returned to the living room with fresh coffee when the power went off without warning. The apartment was suddenly plunged into darkness, and it seemed to heighten the sound of the rain on the rooftop and their isolation from the rest of the world.

"Oh, dear," Pam said in dismay. "I hope the electricity comes back on soon."

"Why?" came the amused voice beside her. "Are you afraid of the dark?"

"Don't be silly!" she replied indignantly. "I'm thinking of the inconvenience to the guests."

"I don't feel inconvenienced at all," Marsh replied.

They had both sat down on the sofa just before the lights went out, but then the wide expanse of the center of the sofa had been between them. Now, Pam became acutely aware of Marsh's nearness. He was so close that her flesh tingled, although he hadn't touched her.

"We have a backup generator system that goes on automatically to power the refrigerated section in the store and at the bait stand, but that's all," Pam said, knowing she was babbling out of nervousness, yet unable to stop herself. "Maybe I ought to go down and open the store. Some of the guests may want to come in to buy flashlights and batteries. I've got some candles in a drawer in the kitchen. I'll just go . . ." She started to rise, but a large hand firmly clasped around her wrist prohibited the action.

"The guests can do without lights for one evening," Marsh said smoothly. "And we really don't need candlelight, do we?" He was so close to her now that he could actually feel her stiffen beside him. It was insane of him . . . he knew it . . . but he still wanted her as much as ever and, though he'd been battling the urge all evening, he couldn't stop himself any longer. He ached to hold her and he buried his face in her sweet-scented, freshly shampooed hair.

Marsh pushed aside the collar of her robe as his lips moved sensually over her bare, silky shoulder. For one long, endless moment Pam froze, and then her heart thudded, out of control like the stormy night itself. A soft warmth made her feel safe, as though she had at last reached a protected place she'd always been seeking, yet at the same time she was as excited and reckless as someone setting out on a daring adventure. For so long she had held herself aloof from feeling anything, knowing that such a route was the path to pain, but she'd been only half a woman. She was so tired of fighting against herself, what she really was; in fact, her whole nature had been carefully and consciously suppressed for years.

The collar slipped farther down her shoulder, exposing more creamy-gold skin. Marsh's lips found her throat as his hands slid around her waist. Pam drew in a small breath, then expelled a soft sigh of surrender. Her own hands went down to cover his and she lifted his right hand to her breast.

Marsh went very still, and a thread of tension wove its way between them.

"Pam?" His voice was hoarse when he finally spoke. "Do you . . . ?"

He broke off, but Pam knew the question all the same. It was the one he'd asked that other night. He wanted her to put her desire for him into words, bold and clear, black and white, so that there could be no misunderstandings.

She twisted slightly in his arms so that she was facing him. In the dark stillness she couldn't see his features, only the darker silhouette of his form contrasting against the soft blue-black shadows that hid the room. Yet she sensed his feelings . . . the anxiety as he awaited her response, and it was that knowledge along with the awakened needs of her body that gave Pam the courage she needed.

Clearing her throat, she lifted her hands to unbutton his shirt. She heard his soft gasp as her fingers slid inside it to touch his warm flesh.

At last she spoke, softly, yet distinctly. "I want you to make love to me, Marsh. I've been so afraid, and maybe I will be again later, but right now the fears are gone and I only know that I want you." A sob rose in her throat, for she was exposing her most secret self to him and there was a danger in that. She was taking a terrible risk that before this evening was over all her self-esteem would be crumbled at her feet, but it was a chance she had to take. For this man. For herself. For them both. She didn't try to reason; she only knew that this was right.

Marsh didn't understand her words about fear, but he recognized the sincerity in her voice. He felt a sudden, overwhelming tenderness toward her, and in that instant her own need to vanquish whatever ghosts there were haunting her was of more importance than his own throbbing desires.

"Darling," he whispered huskily, "it'll be wonderful because I want to show you how very much I care for you. I've never met a sweeter, more desirable woman in my life. All I've thought about since the first day I came here is you."

Pam laughed softly. "You've dominated my thoughts, too," she confessed. "Far too often."

"Correction," Marsh contradicted as he cupped her face with his hands. "I won't be satisfied until I occupy

every one of your thoughts, day and night." He bent
his head and his lips found hers.

There was nothing gentle about the kiss. It was
pressing and demanding, hungry and promising, and it
electrified Pam. A flaming response leaped within her,
and as his mouth forced hers open so that his tongue
could begin an intimate search, her arms went around
his waist and she clung tightly to him as her dizzying
senses spiraled madly.

When Marsh clasped her hand and pulled her to her
feet to lead her into her bedroom, she was aware of a
tingling ache spreading through every cell of her body.

At the edge of the bed, Marsh stopped her and, with
gentle hands, removed her robe so that her nude,
shapely body was silhouetted against the shimmering,
softer blue of the rain-splattered window.

"You're beautiful," he whispered as he bent his head
to kiss her breasts before he lifted her to the bed.

Quickly, he stripped away his own clothes and joined
her. "Now I wish we had lights," he said softly. "I want
to see you, really see you."

"I was just thinking the same thing," Pam said,
emboldened by the unmistakable warmth of his voice.
"You look so magnificent and strong." Her hands
traveled over his hard shoulders and down to his furry
chest.

Marsh's lips claimed hers. One hand slid beneath her
shoulders while his other stroked her breasts and
midsection. When he found her thigh, she shuddered,
giving herself over to the delicious sensations that
suddenly, violently consumed her. Pam had never felt
such searing heat, such pulsating arousal, and the new

and unexpected experience of it was shattering. She no longer felt like herself at all. She lost all sense of reality as she entered another world, a world where she'd never been, a world where pain and pleasure were commingled, a world where passion ruled, where she was filled with the pain of unsatisfied yearnings, where joining was ecstasy beyond comprehension.

Marsh's tongue intimately explored her ear, the hollow at her throat, and finally the thrusting peaks of her nipples. He grew to know her in a way she didn't know herself and brought forth emotions from a depth within her she'd never suspected existed.

She yearned to know his body as thoroughly, and her lips traced the contour of his firm jaw, the angled planes of his shoulders, and down, down his broad, muscular chest, where her fingers embedded themselves in the soft dark hair. Marsh groaned in agony as she made her gentle exploration and his arms wrapped tightly about her.

"I need you," he said raggedly. "Now."

Elation with her newfound and wondrous power over him made Pam shake her head. "Not yet," she whispered. "Not yet." She raked her fingernails along his thigh and felt a spasm rumble through him.

"Woman!" Marsh growled. "I know what you're trying to do! You're trying to torture me to death, right?" Abruptly, he pushed her to the pillows and, as Pam giggled happily, the hard length of his body pressed against hers. "But I can be just as cruel as you!" he threatened.

He proceeded to carry out the threat as he began a fresh assault on her already heightened senses. Pam quivered and moaned as the tension of unreleased pressure rose within her to an unbearable peak.

"Please!" The word tumbled from her lips as she arched toward him. "Please . . . I can't stand any more!"

"I know, darling." Marsh's voice came softly, dreamily. "Neither can I."

They came together in a unison that was as primitive and elemental as the dawn of mankind itself, as explosive as a shooting star, as violent as the storm that even now raged outside and pounded the earth. Pam's heart thundered beneath the weight of Marsh's chest, in perfect tempo with his. He held her closer, ever closer, and she clung to him and buried her face in the crook of his neck, wanting this blazing oneness with him never to end.

When Marsh drew away from her at last to lie beside her with one arm possessively draped across her waist, he looked down at her in the soft darkness and she could actually feel his smile. But almost instantly his demeanor changed; his other hand had gone up to caress her face and he felt the moisture on her cheeks.

"Darling, are those tears?" he asked, astounded.

Pam smiled and lifted her hand to brush it along his cheek. "Happy tears," she said honestly.

Marsh turned his head slightly to kiss the slender hand and then he smiled against it. "It was wonderful," he said with simple satisfaction. "I knew it would be." He paused and, even in the darkness, his gray eyes seemed to glow with an intense fire, warming her. "I love you, you know."

Pam felt no surprise at his words . . . only acceptance, as though she had known all along that it was inevitable, that it was fate, that it had to be. "I know," she said softly. "I love you, too."

Marsh's hand tightened around her waist and she heard the triumphant laughter in his voice. "It took you long enough to realize it," he chided.

"Long!" Pam exclaimed incredulously. "Two weeks? That's about all we've known each other and that's no time at all! That's one of the things that makes me so afraid."

"Hush, darling," Marsh said quietly. "There are about a hundred thousand reasons we could find to make us both afraid of being in love, but I can't think of a one of them worth spoiling this night together." He turned over onto his back, slid one arm beneath her shoulders, and, pulling her into his arms, gently kissed her forehead. "Now just close your eyes and listen while I tell you all the reasons why I love you."

An hour later, long after Marsh's soft, even breathing told her that he was asleep, Pam lay awake in the darkness, listening to the rain. She had not counted on the disruption in her life of falling deeply, irrevocably in love, and now that she had, her heart was heavy and there was no joy in it. She saw only the pain of loss ahead.

Chapter Six

The newly acknowledged feelings between them were so fresh, so young, like the tender budding of a spring leaf or a baby's innocent smile, that both Marsh and Pam were thrown off balance, uncertain about how and where to go with their altered relationship during the next several days.

Pam, of course, was busy running the business, and Marsh kept occupied, too, making himself useful around the place. He took on a couple of major tasks that Gus somehow never found the time to do, like painting the exterior of the store and repairing a desperately needed but given-up-for-dead refrigerator in the storehouse.

Uneasy about accepting his help, Pam reminded Marsh several times that he was supposed to be on a vacation.

While she seemed grateful for what he did, she also appeared to be genuinely distressed about it, despite his reassurances that he was only doing what he really wanted. Marsh couldn't understand her attitude. Why was it so difficult for her to accept a helping hand? Where he came from, you pitched in and helped those you cared about—whether it was your family, your friends, or even your neighbors—and you didn't do it with repayment in mind or with a sense of carrying a burden that was not your own. You just did it because you cared. But Pam obviously saw things differently. He could tell she was worried and even a bit embarrassed about money and that, if she could, she'd have hired extra help to keep up the place. Yet it really bothered her that she couldn't afford to pay him for his work, even though he'd made it as plain as he knew how that he didn't expect it or want it. Somehow she had never learned how to accept favors.

Marsh perched on a stepladder where he was painting brown trim on a window facing of the apartment above the store. The midday sun was blazing, and he tipped back the brim of his cap and rubbed his arm across his perspiring forehead.

Scotty rounded the corner of the building dressed in red swimming trunks and dripping wet. He looked as cool as Marsh felt hot.

"Been in the pool, I see," Marsh commented.

Scotty nodded. "I was diving for pennies with some kids, but their mother made them get out to eat lunch. Mom's got lunch ready too, and she said for you to come."

Marsh nodded. "In a minute. I'm almost done with this window."

Fifteen minutes later, paint-splattered and with his shirt sticking to his back with perspiration, Marsh descended from the ladder and made his way around to the other side of the building to climb the stairs to Pam's apartment. Every day this week since he'd been painting, Pam had insisted upon serving him lunch and dinner. He wished he thought it was only because she wanted to see him and be with him and not because she felt she owed it to him because of the work he was doing, but he couldn't quite kid himself into believing that. Ever since the night they'd slept together, she'd been different in a way he couldn't quite define.

He guessed the best word for it was ambivalent. She seemed to want to be with him and she appeared to enjoy his kisses whenever they happened to snatch a few moments alone together, which, he admitted ruefully to himself, wasn't often. But there was also an odd reserve about her, as though she'd put up some sort of barrier against him; as though, having admitted she loved him, she was now compelled to put a distance between them.

To belie that thought, when he entered the apartment, she came to him immediately and stood on her tiptoes to kiss him. Her action told him louder than words that Scotty wasn't around. Pam had been very insistent that they not display their feelings for each other in front of him or anyone else yet. It was too soon, she'd said, and in that Marsh had agreed with her; once you made other people privy to your personal business, they had a way of taking a proprietorial interest. He wasn't quite ready yet either to have his relationship with Pam examined under a microscope.

Marsh's hand automatically went to Pam's waist as she kissed him, but when she tried to press close to him, he gently shoved her away. "I'm hot and filthy. There's no sense getting you smelly, too." His eyes flickered over her appreciatively. She wore tan, snug-fitting slacks and a pink-and-tan knit shirt that clung nicely to her breasts. Tired as he was, Marsh felt a strong stirring of desire.

Pam saw the burning ardor in his gaze, and a flash of responding arousal overwhelmed her like wildfire. There had been no more evenings like the night when it had stormed because Scotty had been home ever since, and she was surprised at how deprived she felt. She had been cold, iced-over all these years, and it was as though in that one night Marsh had awakened her from a coma. Now she felt vitally alive, utterly feminine and desirable, whole in a way that stunned and amazed her; she had not realized how fragmented she was, and she felt like singing her secret joy to the housetops.

At the same time, she feared the happiness. It was a treacherous thing that lifted her up for the time being, but would surely dash her down again. It wasn't to be trusted; enjoyed for the moment, yes, but never, never to be counted upon to last. The past had taught her about reality. She'd been happy once before in her life, when she married Mike, and that had quickly turned sour. She wasn't to be fooled a second time. This time, caution had to be her watchword. Soon Marsh would be returning to New Orleans, to his family, to his law practice, to his friends and life there that had no connection with hers. For a time, perhaps, he might remember her, still care about her, come to visit her, but their relationship would gradually pull apart, strand by strand, like the frayed threads of old cloth when age and decay take their toll. It was that day for which she had to be prepared.

"Where's Scotty?" Marsh asked.

"He ran down to the mailbox for me," Pam told him. "He'll be back in a minute."

Marsh grinned. "That's what I was afraid of. I was about to suggest I take a quick shower and we forget about lunch."

Pam grinned back sympathetically, and her blue eyes twinkled. "It's a lovely idea, but . . ."

"I know, I know. He'll be back in a minute." Marsh sighed dramatically. "They say the course of true love never runs smooth, and, boy, is that a fact! I doubt if we've even had five minutes alone together all week, and now we've got this camping trip planned with Scotty."

"I don't like it any more than you do," Pam said softly. "It's just been one of those weeks. It seems like everything is conspiring against us." Every day had been packed, as usual, but even the evenings had been unexpectedly busy. One evening she had been committed to go into town to a friend's baby shower; the next, a party of men staying in one of the cabins absolutely insisted upon Marsh's having dinner with them and joining them in a game of poker; and last night she, Marsh, and Scotty, to please Zelma and Gus, had accompanied the older couple to a church cookout. She gave Marsh a devilish grin. "I guess you wouldn't have been so quick to promise to take Scotty camping this weekend if you'd known how the rest of the week was going to be."

Marsh laughed. "No, I guess I wouldn't." He traced a finger along her cheek. "Even so, I wouldn't dare back out now. I'm not sure he'd ever forgive me if I did."

"Scotty *is* excited, all right." Pam smiled at the thought. "It really means a lot to him, Marsh. He's never been camping before."

"So he's told me, and it's high time he did. What time will his friend get here?"

"Jimmy's mother is bringing him out around two this afternoon. What time did you want to leave?"

"Let's shoot for three," Marsh answered. "After lunch, I'll put away the painting supplies and load the truck with the camping gear. Can you get away by then?"

Pam nodded. "Zelma said she'd take over the store whenever I wanted." Aware that time was flying and she was due back downstairs in the store in another half hour so Zelma could go to lunch, she said, "I'd better get our lunch on the table."

Marsh went to the bathroom to wash up, and, by the time he returned, Scotty had come in with the mail and Pam had the chilled chicken salad and iced tea on the table.

In the waning evening light, Pam leaned back against a log and nursed a cup of coffee while she watched contentedly as Marsh and the two small boys scrubbed the tin plates and cooking utensils that had been used for their supper. Not that supper had been elaborate . . . it had consisted of wieners with biscuit dough wrapped around them cooked at the end of a stick over an open fire, and canned fruit. But because the boys had prepared the meal themselves, pride shone in their eyes.

Pam couldn't remember the last time she had ever felt so relaxed . . . or so lazy. Last night and all day today, Marsh had refused to allow her to lift a finger to do anything that smacked of work. He'd made it clear to Scotty and Jimmy as well as to her from the first that she was allowed to do anything she wanted except that. She was not to be permitted to wait upon anyone. They, the "men," a term he applied which delighted two seven-year-old boys, would take care of her this weekend. And they had done just that. With infinite patience that first evening, Marsh had taught the boys how to help him put up the tent; then he had laid out their duties: collecting firewood, building a fire pit. With his guidance, they had cooked all the meals and cleaned up afterwards. And if her hamburger patties or wieners were a little charred or her coffee a bit on the watery side, Pam kept these observations to herself.

"Well, now," she heard Marsh say, "I think that about does it one more time, fellows. Good job! You'd have made some fine frontiersmen, the both of you."

"I wish we could be like Davy Crockett," Jimmy said as he stored away the plates in the cardboard box used for that purpose. "It'd be neat to live out here all the time."

"Yeah, we could even have squirrel stew then, so

long as Mom wasn't around." Scotty glanced toward Pam with teasing scorn. "Back in the olden days, you'd have had to eat it," he informed her.

Pam laughed. All day the boys had begged Marsh to let them try to kill a squirrel for their supper. She had made the appropriate feminine protests and Marsh had refused their request, saying it would be a waste since they'd still have to cook something else for her. It was a good excuse because it kept Marsh from having to give them the real reason, that they were too young to handle the shotgun. Instead, he kept them interested in shooting at tin cans with their BB guns while he stood close by to make sure they handled those safely.

"Sorry, pal," she told him. "I guess I just like my meat to be a little more tame."

"Look, boys," Marsh exclaimed in a hushed voice. "I just saw a rabbit run through that brush over there."

"Let's catch it!" Scotty hissed loudly to Jimmy in what, to him, passed for a whisper.

"Yeah! We might find a whole family of 'em!" Jimmy followed him, and both boys tiptoed off in hot pursuit of the rabbit.

Marsh grinned at Pam, poured himself some black coffee into a tin cup, and sank down beside her. "It's a futile exercise, but it'll probably keep them preoccupied for a good five minutes, at least." He gave a dramatic sigh of weariness.

Pam's eyes danced. "What's the matter? You can't possibly be tired!"

Marsh gave her a pained look as he stretched his legs out in front of him. He grimaced slightly as he adjusted his weak leg into a more comfortable position. "Merely exhausted," he groaned. "Where do they get all that energy? Lord, if we could harness it, we'd have enough to send the astronauts to the moon and back!"

"True," she chuckled softly, "but then we'd have nothing to keep poor grown-ups worn out."

"Not to mention giving us gray hair." Marsh shook his head. "I almost had a coronary this morning when I saw how high Jimmy climbed in that tree. I'd really just as soon not return him to his parents all broken into separate pieces."

Pam shuddered. "Me, too. It was awful enough the time Scotty was visiting Jimmy's family and they had to call and tell me he had cut his foot really bad while he and Jimmy were running barefoot across an open lot. It took ten stitches, and by the time I met them at the doctor's office, I was a nervous wreck, but Scotty wore his bandage like it was a badge of honor." She shook her head. "It gets nerve-wracking sometimes, and then I get to wishing I could just lock him up in his room and not let him out again until he's eighteen." She laughed shakily.

Marsh smiled sympathetically. "I suppose all mothers feel that way to some extent, but I can see how it must be harder on a single mother. It's too bad Scotty's father didn't live to share the responsibility as well as to have the chance to know and enjoy his son. In a way, I feel like an impostor, doing things with him like this camping trip, things that were meant for a boy's real father to have the pleasure of doing with him."

"Don't waste your pity." Pam's voice went hard, and

she averted her face from his so that he couldn't see her face.

"What do you mean?" Marsh sounded genuinely shocked over the change that had come over her.

Pam got to her feet and walked to the campfire. The flames had died down into red-hot burning embers. Her throat felt red-hot, too, with suppressed tears. Pam swallowed hard, moved over to the woodpile, and picked up a heavy branch which she tossed into the coals. Flames leaped up at it, licking greedily, selfishly eager to overpower and consume it. It reminded her of Mike, for he'd been a lot like that. To him, the world had existed only to cater to his every whim, his every mood, and nothing and no one was ever allowed to get in the way of that. Not her, not Scotty.

She whirled around to find that Marsh had risen too. He stood just behind her, gazing thoughtfully at her, concern evident in his eyes.

Her voice had a strident tone to it as she flung the words out, flat and bald. "Mike never wanted Scotty, and from the day he left us until the day he died a few months later, he never bothered to try to see his son again." The bitterness of it all rose up to choke in her throat, and tears salted her eyes, glazing them so that Marsh's face became a shimmering blur.

Marsh did the only thing he knew to do. He gathered her into his arms and pressed her head to his shoulder. "I had no idea," he murmured softly as he stroked her hair. "Whenever Scotty mentions his father, it's always with such pride and respect."

Pam shuddered in his arms. "Of course. I've always

told him how good his father was, how much Mike loved him. I lied to him, Marsh, I lied to him! But what else could I have done?" she cried.

"Shhh!" Marsh dropped tiny kisses to the crown of her head. "You did right. You did what you had to do. Darling, I'm so sorry."

Pam sniffed and, regaining some semblance of control, gave a small, unsteady laugh. "Yes," she whispered. "I'm sorry, too . . . for Scotty. But I'll never tell him the real truth. No child should be punished with that!"

"I agree with you," Marsh said quietly. He held her slightly away from him so that she could see the tender smile in his eyes. "But listen to me, Pam . . . there are all sorts of ways to tell the truth. You're telling Scotty the real truth of your love for him by shielding him from the other. Don't ever be sorry for that. It just shows what a warm, caring woman you are." The smile in his eyes spread to his lips. "By the way, did I mention to you today that I happen to love you?"

Pam found an answering smile. "I don't believe you did." She lifted her face for a kiss. "Why don't you tell me now?"

"The rabbit got away!" a young, disgruntled voice said nearby. Pam started guiltily and withdrew from Marsh's embrace. But it wasn't soon enough. Scotty had seen them together. He approached them now, his face curious. "Why were you holding my mother?" he asked Marsh. There was no resentment in the question, merely interest.

Marsh looked at Pam and at the brief shake of her

head, and said easily, "A cinder from the fire got into her eye. I was helping her get it out."

"Oh."

Scotty lost interest as Jimmy came into sight and announced, "I'm hungry."

Pam had to laugh at the incredulous expression on Marsh's face. "How can you possibly be hungry?" he demanded. "I watched you wolf down five hotdogs an hour ago!"

"I'm hungry too," Scotty said. "Can we roast some marshmallows?"

The remainder of the evening passed pleasantly. The two boys entertained themselves for a time catching fireflies and storing them in an empty mayonnaise jar with holes poked through the lid. Later Marsh taught them an absurd song about a frog on a log in the bottom of the sea. With each new stanza, it became longer and more complicated, so that they all kept forgetting parts of it and breaking off amid giggles and laughter. Pam loved the contrast between the deep, rich baritone of Marsh's voice and the high-pitched young voices of the boys, and she listened with a smile every time she became hopelessly tangled in the lines and stopped singing herself. However, each time she did, Marsh would soon realize she wasn't carrying her weight and would stop in the middle of the song to order sternly, "Sing! You'll get no breakfast tomorrow if you don't sing!"

Finally the youngsters grew sleepy, and Marsh supervised their washing up before they crawled into their sleeping bags inside the tent.

Pam and Marsh remained by the fire, and he put his arm around her and drew her head down to rest against his shoulder. A slight breeze had sprung up and the night air was silky and cool. The wind rustled gently through the trees, almost lovingly, as though it were caressing every leaf, every pine bough. It nudged at the flames in the fire so that they flared, blue and gold, dancing with exotic frenzy before erupting into showers of orange and red sparks.

Marsh lifted his head, gazing up at the few stars that could be seen between the treetops. "It's sort of like being in a little corner of heaven here," he sighed. "Lovely and peaceful."

"Ummmm," Pam murmured. "I'm not sure I ever want to return to reality."

Marsh's hand tightened on her shoulder. "This *is* reality," he insisted softly. "All this beauty, us here together. It's never going to end."

"Everything ends sometime," Pam said somberly. She turned her head so that she could look up at him. The glow of firelight reflected in his eyes. "It feels so strange," she told him. "Being happy."

Marsh's lips softened into a smile. "I know," he said quietly. "I'm not used to it, either." The smile turned into an engaging grin. "But maybe with a little practice, we can adjust."

He lowered his head, and Pam lifted hers, welcoming his kiss. It was only when Marsh held her close that her doubts and fears subsided, merging into the dark shadowy places of her mind and leaving her, for a time, in the brilliant sunlit landscape of Marsh's love. She was still surprised, awed by the incredible thing that had happened to her the night they'd made love. Without even knowing it, he'd proved to her that mutual passion really existed . . . that she could both give and receive within the realm of physical love. It was a priceless and glorious discovery.

Marsh's hand slid beneath Pam's shirt and up to cover a breast. Her breath caught at the warm, tingling yearning he created in her. Her lips parted beneath the hungry fierceness of his kiss while her own hands raked his back.

"Damn clothes," Marsh muttered as his hand went down and encountered the stiff waistband of her jeans. "I want to make love to you."

"I know," Pam whispered unsteadily. "I know." She tugged at his shirt and freed it from the waistband of his jeans and buried her hands beneath the fabric, loving the sensation of touching the warm flesh of his back. "I . . . I want it too."

Marsh began to unbutton her shirt and when it fell open, his hands went round to her back, about to unhook her bra. The searing heat of his gaze brought a surge of color to her face, warming her more thoroughly than the nearby fire. Pam's heart began to thunder in anticipation.

"Mom! *Mom!*"

Abruptly, they both crashed back to earth. A little dazed, Pam met Marsh's eyes and recognized the frustration she saw in them. It was her own as well.

"What is it, Scotty?" she called back, her eyes never leaving Marsh's face. "Can't you sleep?"

"I've got a stomachache."

Marsh's hands dropped away from her, and Pam

hastily did up the buttons on her shirt. "I'm coming," she said loudly to Scotty, and to Marsh, in a whisper, "I'm sorry."

His smile was rueful. "So am I." He got to his feet and helped her up. "You'd better go to him. I'll just put out the fire."

Marsh was awake at dawn the following morning. For a while he lay still, enjoying the hushed quiet, the expectant silence of a new day. Nothing stirred. Even the birds and insects and small animals that lived in these woods were still sleeping.

After a time, he turned over onto his side and opened his eyes. The two small boys lay beside him, young and innocent and sweet in their slumber. Jimmy was curled up into a tight knot, and his head was almost completely buried beneath the cover. Scotty, though, was sprawled everywhere, all arms and legs. One leg was tucked beneath the covers, but the rest of him was on top of his sleeping bag and even his arms were wide-flung. His tousled hair flopped over one closed eye.

Marsh's gaze traveled on to Pam, who slept on the opposite side of the tent. She was stretched out almost full length, with only her knees slightly bent as she lay on her side facing toward him. One arm was tucked beneath her pillow, the other resting on top of the sleeping bag. She looked serene and peaceful in her sleep.

A knot lodged in Marsh's throat. He felt a protective tenderness come over him as he observed them all. It must be, he thought, the way a man feels about his family; he went all soft inside at such a sight, having a fierce desire to keep them safe and out of harm's way.

But they weren't his family. They didn't belong to him. No one did. The intrusive thought unsettled him, and Marsh quietly crawled out of his bag, still fully dressed, picked up his boots, and, opening the tent flap, went outside into the gray, early morning.

He built a fire and soon had the coffee going. Then he poured some water into a washpan and doused his face. His chin was raspy with the stubble of an overnight beard as his hands brushed over it. He would shave after breakfast. For the moment he contented himself with washing his face and brushing his teeth.

When the coffee was ready, he poured some into a tin cup, then hunkered down beside the fire, staring into it as though it mesmerized him. But his thoughts were on the ones he'd left inside the tent.

Marsh lifted his head and looked around the clearing in the woods. Pines dominated here, but there were a few gum and oak as well. To his left, a quarter of a mile off, the land ended as it came to the banks along Toledo Bend Reservoir. Gus had told him he was considering selling the land, and Marsh squinted against the morning light as he pondered whether or not to buy it. There were over forty acres here and it would make a wonderful homesite.

He hadn't mentioned anything to Pam yet about the possibility of his buying it, mainly because he hadn't been sure in his own mind whether he really wanted it or not. There was so much to consider. Did he really want to move here and make a permanent home, or would it be better just to build a vacation-type cabin, a place to visit on weekends while he still lived and maintained a practice in New Orleans? Or was it better to simply forget the whole thing?

The main consideration really was where Pam fit into any plans he made. He loved her with a depth that astonished him, she claimed she loved him. All the same, as she'd pointed out the other night, in reality they scarcely knew one another. There were so many things that had gone into making them the people they were that neither one of them understood about the other. As they grew to know each other better, would the love endure?

Love, as far as Marsh had experienced it, hadn't had much of a track record for longevity, and the last thing he wanted was more failure. He wanted marriage, children of his own, a relationship that would last the rest of his life, but how could you really know for sure?

They hadn't discussed the subject of marriage, and he didn't know how Pam felt about it. Hell, he didn't even know whether she would want any more children even if she wanted marriage. After all, she'd already had the fulfillment of motherhood; she had Scotty. She was a good mother and she loved him, but that was no argument that she might want more children, and Marsh knew that fond as he was of her son, that wasn't enough for him. He would want his own flesh and blood, too.

Yet the only alternatives were also unsatisfying. They could live together, merely have an affair, or stop seeing each other. Marsh didn't like any of them. Living together might offer a semblance of marriage, but it would be but a pale shadow of what he really wanted. An affair without living together would be equally unfulfilling. He really couldn't see himself going on very long juggling things just to sneak a few hours with her. And finally, the thought of never seeing her at all was even more unsupportable than the others. He'd only known her a short time, yet he couldn't even visualize going back to the same existence he'd had before the accident, picking up where he left off just as though she'd never come into his life. It had seemed like a fairly good life then; now it stretched before him like a desert wasteland if Pam wasn't in it with him.

The object of these intense thoughts came out of the tent just then. As she stood just in front of the flap in the same jeans and shirt she'd worn the day before and with her short dark hair in disarray, Marsh thought she'd never looked more appealing. Her face had the freshness of youth after her night's sleep; it was devoid of any makeup whatsoever, and her lovely blue eyes were wide and bright.

"Good morning," Marsh said with a smile. He got to his feet. "I didn't wake you, did I?"

Pam smiled back. "Maybe you did. Maybe at a subconscious level I knew you were gone and I didn't like it."

Marsh laughed softly. "I think I like the way your subconscience works," he said. "Want some coffee?"

She nodded. "It smells good."

While he poured it for her, she washed up and, returning to join him near the fire, threaded her fingers through her hair, trying to tame it. "I couldn't find my comb," she said ruefully, "and I was afraid if I kept searching, I'd wake up the time bombs."

Marsh grinned and handed her the coffee. "You look beautiful," he told her in a soft voice.

"Yes?" Pam tilted her head to one side and eyed him sharply. "I see we need to have your eyes examined as soon as we get back to civilization. They're obviously in very bad shape."

"I have twenty-twenty vision," he returned. "The malady I'm suffering from can't possibly be healed by a pair of eyeglasses."

"What's that?" she asked with a tiny smile playing across her lips.

"I'm in love," he said in a tone of complaint. "Worst disease I've ever had."

Pam laughed and went to him, lifting her face to kiss him. His lips were soft on hers, his overnight growth of beard scratchy against her cheek. She backed away slightly and ran her hand lovingly across the stubbly dark growth. "I have the same terrible condition," she teased as she looked up and basked in the warmth of the light in his eyes. "I wonder if medical science has discovered a cure for it yet?"

Marsh shook his head. "Nope. It's in the same category as the common cold. All you can do is tough it out. Trouble is, this kind of illness lingers on and on."

"Hmmm. I wonder what we should do to alleviate the symptoms."

"How about getting married?" Marsh asked casually.

The abrupt change that came over Pam was astounding to him. Her hand dropped away from his face and her entire body went rigid while the color flowed out of her face.

"You're . . . you're joking, right?" she asked finally in a raspy voice.

"It's not a joke I'm in the habit of making," Marsh said, watching her closely. "There's always the danger the wrong person could take it seriously."

"I never dreamed, I never expected . . . I don't know what to say," she whispered at last.

Marsh's jaw clenched. Her reaction was certainly not one he had anticipated, and he felt a stab of deep disappointment. "Say yes or no," he told her. "It was a straightforward sort of question. Either you want to marry me or you don't."

Pam struggled to breathe. She had a helpless, sickening sensation, as though chains were being wrapped about her, tightening, choking her, suffocating her. The wonderfully free exhilaration of loving him was now reduced to iron bars of imprisonment. And she couldn't let that happen to her, not again.

Tears of wild frustration burned in her eyes and throat and she longed to hit out at something, anything, even Marsh himself. Still balancing the tin cup of coffee in one hand, she knotted the other at her side and sucked in a deep breath. "Why did you have to spoil it?" she asked bitterly. "Oh, Marsh, why did you have to go and spoil it?"

Marsh blanched, his face as white as her own. "I didn't know I was spoiling anything," he said distantly.

"I only thought it was the next logical step for us. I love you; you know I'm crazy about Scotty and I'd try to be a good father to him. I want children of my own . . . your children. What's so terrible about that?"

"It's impossible, that's all!" she cried distractedly. Pam pushed her hair back from her brow and turned away from him in agitation. "You're pushing me, Marsh," she said in a voice that trembled. "You want things your own way, but I won't do it! No man will ever again have such power over me!"

"What power?" She heard the incredulity in his voice. "Who said anything about power? All I want is a marriage, a family, a home for God's sake!"

Pam's shoulders slumped as she stared down into the fire. "A man's home is his castle, after all!" She choked over the words. She whirled toward him and her eyes blazed with resentment. "No, thank you, Marsh. I tried it once, but I'll not be a wench in any man's castle ever again! I intend to run my own life as I see fit without answering to anyone!"

"I see," Marsh said coldly. "What you really mean is that you're too self-centered to share your life. I hadn't seen that side of you before. Well, fine, lady. Now is the moment of truth. I'm glad we had this little chat and cleared the air so I won't bother wasting any more of my time on someone who was wrong for me all along!" He moved toward the ice chest and opened it. "I'll get breakfast started. As soon as the boys are up and we've eaten, we'll break camp and head back."

Pam swallowed the tears that clogged her throat. She felt dreadful, as though she were ill, and her whole body was quivering with the pain of losing him. Yet he left her no choice. No choice at all.

Slowly, she turned toward him and, trying to keep her voice as steady and reasonable as possible, she said huskily, "I . . . I'd appreciate it if, for the remainder of the time you're staying at the resort, you'd ease yourself away from Scotty. He . . . he likes you so much—" here her voice broke slightly and she nibbled at her lower lip to still it before continuing—"and it's going to be hard on him when you go away. There's no sense making it any harder."

"That should be easy enough," Marsh said in a harsh voice unlike any she'd ever heard before. "I'll be packing up and moving out just as soon as we get back."

"I . . . I see." Pam fought the aching pain that had invaded every cell of her body. "Maybe that would be best."

Two hours later Marsh deposited Pam and two confused little boys at Pam's apartment. The children naturally could not understand why they had to hurry back this morning, since the night before Marsh had been planning to teach them how to lash together a makeshift table out of fallen branches. In brutal silence, he left it to Pam to make excuses, which she did by firmly insisting that she'd remembered some important work she had to do that could not be put off. By careful omission, she did not mention the fact that Marsh would be going away today.

Finally alone in his cabin, Marsh relieved only a minute amount of his fury by storming from room to room, violently throwing his belongings into a suitcase and cardboard boxes, not caring how haphazardly the job was done. The quicker he could get away from here, he thought, the better. The raw pain in every cell spurred him onward without pause. Only when he was away from here entirely would he be able to begin to find a way to anesthetize it.

Chapter Seven

Zelma, who was minding the store, was surprised to see Pam back so early, but frankly delighted that she was.

"My sister and her husband came down this morning from Lafayette to stay a couple of days with us. Since you're back early, it'll give me more time to spend with them."

"Of course." Pam glanced down at her wrinkled clothes. "Just give me half an hour to shower and change," she pleaded, "and then I'll relieve you."

Zelma nodded agreeably. "There's no hurry. My sister knows how to make herself at home. She's probably already got dinner started. By the way," she asked belatedly, "how was your camp-out?"

"Fine," Pam answered hastily. "Fine. The boys loved it." She was relieved to see customers entering the store so that she had an excuse to drop the subject. "I'll run upstairs now," she added. "I'll be back in a few minutes."

She wished she didn't have to take over the store so soon. Marsh would be checking out, and Pam had counted on it being Zelma, not herself, who dealt with him about that. Normally Zelma was available to pitch in for her any time she needed her. It was rotten timing that today of all days she should need to rush away.

In the privacy of the shower, Pam let the tears she'd been holding back flow freely. She ached with despair at the knowledge that something fine and wonderful was being lost to her. Yet the very thought of being trapped in a marriage again caused her to shudder. People talked so much about women being liberated these days. Well, she was liberated . . . *now.* But the idea of liberation within marriage was a myth, a bad, tasteless joke, and now that she had experienced real freedom, she wouldn't, couldn't ever allow herself to be dominated and subjected to the indignity of that sort of imprisonment again.

How could people of conscience speak of the sanctity of marriage? she wondered as she soaped herself. Her memories of childhood, before her parents' divorce, were of them screaming and yelling at each other. With Mike, the yelling had been all on one side. He had yelled; she had listened, hoping if she didn't argue things would soon calm down. Yet no matter how hard she had tried to anticipate his desires, no matter how much she tried to please, he had never really been satisfied. He had even kept her on a strict allowance.

My God, she groaned now beneath the spray of hot water, *allowance!* Just as though she'd been a child like Scotty. Even worse, she'd had to account to him for where each penny of that money had gone, right down to each pack of chewing gum or a magazine! Mike hadn't minded buying things he wanted—he'd worn the best clothes and he'd loved to buy electronic gadgets like expensive tape decks, even a ham radio. Yet once when she'd had the flu and had gone to the doctor when Mike hadn't felt she'd really needed to, he'd been so incensed by the pharmacy bill that he had cut back on her allowance, saying she obviously didn't need so much money if she was going to waste it like that on an illness that wasn't serious. Another time, when Scotty was a few weeks old, she had taken him to a photography studio to have his portrait made, and there had been another bad scene over that. Throughout their marriage Mike had kept rigid control over the money, and then when he left her . . .

Pam pushed away the thought of the embarrassment and shame of that time. Anyway, what was the point of dredging up such painful memories except as a reminder not to place herself in such a predicament again.

No, she thought as she patted herself with perfumed dusting powder after her shower, she'd done the right thing, the only possible thing by refusing Marsh's proposal. There was no other way to retain her hard-won self-respect as well as her precious freedom. To give up such treasures would be like giving up breathing itself.

Yet some deeper, inner core of her being cried out in

protest. *You're being a fool,* it said. *He's the other half of yourself,* it said. *How will you bear the loneliness once he's gone?* it asked.

Marsh had given new meaning to the term "love" for her. He had opened a previously barred door for her, bringing her to a wondrous joy and appreciation of her womanhood, teaching her by example the definition of fulfillment, enriching the very essence of her being. When he left, all her brief, newfound happiness would be going with him.

It wasn't fair, her heart cried. Why had she been tantalized by that which was ultimately to be denied her?

But if she had only looked ahead, she should have seen it coming. Not his marriage proposal; that had been entirely unexpected. But logic told her that whatever the relationship that was developing between them, it had, of necessity to come to an end once he returned to his real life in New Orleans. The trouble was that she hadn't thought; or more precisely, hadn't wanted to think or to see that far. She'd been too caught up in the thrill of the present, in the sensuously explosive feelings between them, and she hadn't spared a thought to anything beyond the present.

Pam finished dressing, ran down the stairs, and, after checking on the two boys who were playing behind the building with Scotty's dog Rusty, went into the store. Five minutes later Zelma left, and Pam took over and waited on customers.

Afterwards, when the other customers had gone, a handsome couple who seemed vaguely familiar to Pam came inside the store. They were neatly dressed in casual shorts and shirts, and both of them appeared to be in their early thirties.

"Hi," the man said with a flash of teeth as he smiled easily. "I'm Dick Palmer, and this is my wife, Janet. I called last week and made reservations for a cabin."

"Just a moment and I'll look it up for you," Pam replied. She found the right paper and nodded. "For a week, is that right, Mr. Palmer?"

"That's right." He leaned lazily against the counter. "It's been a couple of years since we were last here," he said idly. "I hope our catches are as good this week as they were then."

"So you have been here before?" Pam asked, smiling. "I thought you looked familiar. As for the fishing" —she shrugged—"it's hard to say. Some of our guests have been bringing in some terrific catches, but others have complained about their lack of luck."

Dick Palmer grinned. "Same old story. What sort of luck has Marsh Franklin been having, do you know?"

"Marsh Franklin?" Pam echoed weakly. Her fingers froze around the pencil she gripped, and she stared at him as though he were speaking an unfamiliar foreign language.

"We're friends of his," the woman beside him explained. "In fact, we're the ones who told him about this place." She stopped abruptly and looked at Pam with a strange expression in her brown eyes. "Is there anything wrong?" she asked. "Marsh *is* staying here, isn't he?"

The odd way the woman looked at her finally made Pam aware that she must have been staring. "Er . . . yes. Yes, he's here."

"Good." The man chuckled. "We didn't tell him we were coming. We thought we'd surprise him."

"I . . . see," Pam said slowly, realizing at once that the couple would do more than surprise him. They were also going to upset his plans to leave right away. The break would not be so clean and swift after all. "He . . . ummm . . . he'll be surprised, all right. I'm sure he'll be delighted to see you."

Palmer laughed heartily. " 'Delighted' might be a little strong," he told her. "But I imagine he'll be glad to see a couple of familiar faces after being here alone for three weeks."

"Don't be silly, darling," his wife said, eyeing Pam shrewdly. "I doubt he's exactly spent all his time here *alone.*"

The penetrating look in her gaze caused Pam's face to warm. The woman was fishing for information Pam was not about to give, and, to hide both her embarrassment and swift surge of annoyance over the other woman's curiosity, she glanced down at the papers before her on the counter. "If you'll just sign here, Mr. Palmer, I'll get your . . ."

"Jan! Dick, you old son-of-a-gun, I don't believe this! What are you two doing here?"

All eyes turned toward the door, where Marsh stood shaking his head in disbelief.

"Same as you," Palmer said as he and Marsh pounded each other's shoulders. "We came for a little fishing and relaxation. We also came to keep you company. Figured you might be getting a little lonesome about now."

"It's great to see you!" Marsh wrapped his arms

around Janet Palmer in a fond bear hug and Pam swallowed hard over the jealousy that suddenly clogged her throat. The fact that the other woman was married and her husband was beaming with approval mattered not at all. She was absolutely trembling with rage and envy!

"How's the fishing been?" Dick asked when Marsh had released his wife.

"Fair. I've had a couple of really nice-sized large-mouth bass."

He half-turned his back to the counter and Pam was sure he did it deliberately so that he wouldn't have to acknowledge her, wouldn't have to include her in the conversation. Rigidly, she turned her own back to the counter, filed away the Palmers' reservation slip, and got their cabin key. She placed it on the counter and then went to sit down at the small desk in the corner, pretending to become engrossed in the paperwork there.

"We're counting on you to show us the best fishing holes this week," Janet Palmer said. "As long as you've been here, you ought to know them all by now."

"Sure," Marsh responded agreeably. "My pleasure. Are you finished here?" he asked briskly in a different tone of voice. "Why don't you get settled into your cabin and then we'll all drive into Many for lunch. Tomorrow morning first thing, we'll get busy catching those fish."

"Sounds great. This my key, miss?" Dick Palmer asked, peering down at Pam where she sat partially hidden from view.

"Yes, sir. To reach your cabin, take the second left

down the road, then left again. Your cabin will be the third on your right." She mustered something that passed for a smile. "I hope you'll enjoy your stay with us."

"I'm sure we will." He followed his wife out the door. "Coming, Marsh?" he asked.

"In a minute," Marsh replied. "I'll catch up with you at your cabin."

The other couple climbed into their car. Inside the store there was a pregnant silence until the car slowly pulled out of the driveway to move down the gravel road.

Pam sat behind the counter, scarcely breathing. She waited for Marsh to say something and finally, when she heard a noise and looked up, she saw that he had walked around the counter. His eyes were dark and glazed with such unhappiness that she almost cried.

"I suppose I'll be staying on for another week after all," he said reluctantly, as though he hated every word. "It's either that or answer a lot of damned awkward questions, besides disappointing my friends."

Pam inclined her head. "I understand," she said quietly.

"Thanks." Marsh's voice was strained. "Thanks for not giving me away. It could have been a bit embarrassing if my friends knew you'd dumped me."

"Marsh!" Pam cried. She got to her feet and moved toward him, her hand outstretched. "I didn't do that! I love you! It's just . . ."

"We've been over that ground once already and I don't feel in the mood to cover it again," Marsh said harshly. "You don't want to marry me, it's as simple as that! But don't waste your breath trying to convince me you love me. I honestly don't think you understand the meaning of the word."

"That's not fair, Marsh! I . . ."

"Fair?" he ground out. "What's fair got to do with anything? Anything at all?" He sighed heavily and said in a more reasonable tone of voice, "I'll try to stay out of your way this week, Pam, so that it'll be as painless as possible for both of us."

It was one of the most difficult weeks Pam ever recalled enduring. An air conditioner in one of the cabins had to be replaced. She had a flat tire on the highway one afternoon when she'd been returning from Many and she'd had to walk a mile and a half to reach a telephone so she could call Gus. There was also a waterline break which left the resort and nearby residents without running water for almost two whole days. Pam then had to buy a large supply of bottled water just to keep things going and the guests placated.

In addition, the dull, relentless heartache over Marsh persisted. True to his word, he stayed away from her, though she often saw him at a distance with his friends. If something were needed from the store, however, it was always Janet or Dick Palmer who came for it . . . never Marsh.

Even with his still staying at the resort, it might have been a bit easier for Pam if it hadn't been for Scotty. He still saw as much of Marsh as ever, and Pam didn't have the heart anymore to discourage it. After all, in just a few more days Marsh would be walking out of their lives for good; Scotty was going to miss him terribly as it was, so what good would it have done to keep him from Marsh for the little time remaining for them to see each other?

On Thursday, for the second time that week, Marsh invited Scotty to join him and the Palmers on their fishing excursion, and Pam readily assented. She knew Marsh would take good care of her son and she just couldn't deny him the pleasure.

Late that afternoon a phone call came for Marsh. Pam took the message and, after she closed the store at five-thirty, she walked down to the pier to wait.

She sank to the pier, crisscrossing her jeaned legs and closing her eyes, letting the warmth of the late afternoon sun and the gentle breeze drift over her. The water slapped softly against the pier and around the pilings and boat hulls, and to Pam the rhythmic sound was soothing.

She felt tired, drained of energy, and she knew it was a combination of overwork, financial worries, and her unhappiness over the current situation with Marsh. She had slept badly all week.

Was she, in fact, being a fool for refusing to marry him? The sexual tension in her body whenever she thought of his lovemaking told her she was. So did her heart, as it reminded her of the soft teasing glow that came to his eyes whenever he was in a playful mood; the infectious smile; the kindness he showed toward others out of sheer generosity. Marriage to such a man ought to be a dream come true.

He wanted to be a father to her children, he'd said. Certainly he was good to Scotty, and if that were a true indication of how he'd be within a family structure, he'd make a terrific father. For a long, dangerous moment Pam allowed herself to lapse into a daydream. They both had dark hair, so their children would, too, of course, but would they have her blue eyes or his gray ones, her freckles or his darker complexion? He'd been so pale when he'd first come here a month ago, but now his skin was a healthy golden color like a ripe apricot. Pam visualized Marsh standing at her hospital bedside, holding their firstborn in his arms while he wore a silly grin of awe and bliss on his face.

Abruptly, the vision blurred and faded. That was only a scene out of the movies and she was kidding herself if she wasted even an instant believing in it. She'd already been through the real thing, Pam reminded herself bitterly. How could she be so foolish as to imagine a second time—or a second husband— would be any different? Marriage was only a nightmare, not a dream come true. Kindness could quickly turn to cruel selfishness, and just because Marsh said he wanted children, it didn't necessarily follow that if it actually happened, he'd be any happier about the intrusion in his life than Mike had been. Certainly Mike had never grinned ridiculously over Scotty's birth.

Through the haze of her painful thoughts, Pam heard the putt-putt of an engine. She opened her eyes, squinting against the western orange-streaked sky, and saw Marsh's boat round the bend and come into view across the open channel.

A moment later it was near enough so that the occupants were recognizable. Scotty, outstanding in his bright-orange life vest, waved vigorously.

"Hi, Mom!" he shouted.

Pam waved back and got to her feet as the boat approached the dock, swung into position, and nosed into the slip.

Only then did Marsh glance up and, as Pam reached out, obviously offering to catch the rope to tie off his boat, he suddenly smiled at her. Instantaneous joy rolled over her in a billowing wave, surging against her ribs and breaking around her heart into a fine spray like shimmering droplets of water.

Her eyes were suddenly moist as her lips softened into an answering smile. For a timeless moment, as long as eternity, as brief as a pulsebeat, they gazed at each other. Within the gaze, they were in a world of their own, a place that included no others as it sheltered them from all else. The inlet of water, the boats, the pier, even Marsh's companions, Scotty and the Palmers, faded and became invisible.

Pam's gaze traveled over Marsh with hungry greed. He wore tight-fitting jeans and a red plaid sports shirt, open at the throat. The power of his muscles was plainly visible as he moved, both in his thighs and arms. She felt a hot tingling of desire, a fierce longing to touch him, and it was such a strong impulse that she actually trembled from the wanting.

Her eyes met his again, and at once she saw that something had changed. The same desire she had felt had been clearly reflected in the soft gray mirror of his eyes, but now that was gone. The eyes became slate-gray, distant, withdrawn. Indifference, worse even than anger or hatred, had taken its place.

"Ready?" she heard him ask in a steady voice that contained no hint of emotion of any sort.

Pam swallowed with difficulty, blinked rapidly to clear her cloudy vision, and nodded. Marsh tossed her the rope, and she gripped it hard, bracing one leg against the piling while Marsh leaped from the boat to the pier like a graceful stag skimming over the top of a fence.

He came to her at once, his body brushing hers as his strong brown hands took the rope from her grasp. An electric jolt went through her at the contact, and she heard Marsh utter a small gasp beneath his breath before their gazes met once again. Something Pam could not quite interpret flickered in Marsh's eyes, but then the moment was gone as Marsh spoke coolly. "Thanks. I can take over now."

Pam snatched her own hands away and backed off a step, all at once acutely aware of their audience. By that time, Scotty and the Palmers were standing on the pier, watching them.

"Look what we caught, Mom!" Scotty said proudly.

Pam turned in his direction, relieved at the timely distraction. Scotty was struggling to hold up a stringer of fish that was almost as long as he was. There were numerous crappie, a few bluegill, and a couple of striped bass.

"My goodness!" Pam found a smile. "It looks as though you did pretty well for yourselves. I should have brought along my camera to add a photo of your catch to the bulletin board," she said, referring to the large display along one wall in the store. It was covered with photographs from past fishing tournaments as well as other occasions when guests brought in noteworthy catches. It was a favorite browsing spot, especially for first-time newcomers.

"As usual, the camera-worthy ones got away," Dick Palmer said with a rueful grin. "Marsh almost caught a trophy-sized striper, though. I swear that thing weighed at least twenty-five pounds! It was a beaut! Unfortunately, the line got snagged on some underwater brush and he broke loose."

"Did you use a lure or baitfish?" Pam asked Marsh as he joined them, glad to be on a safe, everyday subject. It served to help her get her balance again, to speak normally after the terrible tension that had gripped her moments before.

"Bluegill," Marsh replied in the same casual tone she had just used. He smiled down at Scotty. "Want me to take that?" he asked. "It looks like it might be getting just a little heavy for you."

Scotty relinquished the stringer with their catch and looked at his mother. "We're gonna have a fish fry tonight. It's okay if I eat supper with them, isn't it?"

Janet Palmer smiled pleasantly at Pam. "We'd love to have you join us, too," she said cordially. "Scotty contributed as much to the meal as any of us, and as you can see, there's plenty."

Pam appreciated the invitation. During the week, the few times Janet had come into the store for something and they had chatted, the two of them had become quite friendly. Pam's initial, unreasonable dislike of Janet because of her curiosity about her relationship with Marsh, not to mention the pure envy that had seized her when Marsh had hugged his friend, was gone. She really liked Janet a lot, and if it weren't for her close association with Marsh, they could probably have become good friends themselves. But no matter how much she liked the other woman, Pam had tried all week to maintain a certain distance, sharply aware that Janet was Marsh's friend first and that, given the circumstances, it was better all around if they didn't grow too close.

Now, with her back to Marsh, she felt a prickling chill. His eyes were on her, and she was conscious of his waiting stillness. Her nerves tightened. What did he want? she wondered in agony. Did he want her to accept the invitation or to stay away?

The past few days provided the answer. Marsh had avoided her all week. Despite that compelling gaze the two of them had shared moments ago, it was clear that he didn't want to be around her. They were far too aware of each other to maintain a facade of careless indifference for very long in front of others. It would be too exhausting, too nerve-wracking for them both.

"Thanks a lot," she said evenly as she kept her eyes on Janet, "but I'd better not. I've got some bookwork to do. However, it's fine with me if Scotty joins you. It's nice of you to include him."

Janet laughed and, with a fond gesture, ruffled Scotty's hair. "Don't be silly. He was the only gallant gentleman of the bunch today. He baited my hook for me. As far as I'm concerned," she added, cutting her eyes meaningfully toward the two men, "Scotty's the only man here who deserves a good meal!"

Scotty's face split into a grin. "She couldn't stand to hold the crickets," he explained. "She said they're too squiggly."

Pam laughed. "I'm glad you helped a lady in distress."

Dick Palmer sighed dramatically. "The only way we're possibly going to redeem ourselves, Marsh, is by cleaning the fish. We'd better get busy."

"Right," Marsh said. "But if Sir Walter Raleigh here thinks he's going to get out of the dirty work, he's mistaken. Now, listen up, Scotty. I don't care what Janet says; if you don't help us clean these fish, you'll get no supper tonight."

Scotty giggled. "Okay, I'll help. What about Janet? Doesn't she have to help, too?"

Janet wrinkled her nose at him and, in the vernacular, declared fervently, "Them that cooks, don't clean."

While the others began straggling down the pier, Marsh hesitated as he looked once more at Pam's stiff back. She was gazing into the distance as though the water and the setting sun mesmerized her. He nearly went to her, but then he restrained himself, sighing wearily. For a moment when they'd first arrived, there had been something in her eyes that had sparked new hope in him. But it had been quickly extinguished, and he had felt a deep stab of disappointment when she'd refused Janet's invitation to join them for dinner.

Not that he had really expected a different answer. Why would she want to be near him, to be reminded of the fiasco he'd made of things? Only a fool would rush a relationship the way he'd done. No one in their right mind would jump at a marriage proposal after knowing someone only a few short weeks . . . especially the second time around. A part of him wanted to tell her he understood, to seek to reestablish the relationship they'd had before he'd made his big blunder. Maybe if they took things slow and easy, really got to know one another, she would change her mind.

But there was something else that kept him silent. Pam had been so adamant. It wasn't only that they had known each other such a short time. She had been against marriage, period. The memory of her reaction that day in the woods did away with any urge to go back to where they had been. What was the point? He loved her and wanted her, and right now, just seeing her made him ache with a desperate longing to hold her, but if she didn't want to make any commitments in her life, sooner or later, somewhere down the line, he would have to learn to do without her for good. It might as well be now as later, Marsh reasoned, because the longer he was with her, the more pain the ultimate break would bring.

At last, Marsh turned away, slowly following the others down the pier, but he had only taken a few steps when Pam called his name. He stopped, waiting for her to catch up with him, and a tightness squeezed his chest. He hoped . . . He crushed down the thought.

"I nearly forgot why I came down to wait for you," Pam said apologetically. She pulled a scrap of paper from a hip pocket of her jeans. "You had a phone call from your office today and they want you to call back in the morning. Something to do with the Trahan case you were working on before your accident."

The hope that had still been alive in his heart died. Marsh took the paper and stuffed it into his shirt pocket. "Thanks," he said brusquely. While handing him the paper, Pam's shoulder had brushed against his arm. The intimate contact was sheer torture, and it made him sound more gruff than he'd intended. "Fine. I'll do that."

Their eyes met, and Marsh saw hurt welling up in Pam's gaze before it was quickly masked. It seemed to him that her shoulders squared, her chin rising. She nodded briefly, then moved away, striding briskly ahead.

Damn! Marsh thought savagely. It seemed all they did was continually hurt each other, in large ways, in numerous small ways, even without intending to do it. The sooner distance was put between them, the sooner the healing process could begin.

But meantime, he was stuck at the resort until Sunday, when the Palmers would be going home. Marsh toyed with the idea of leaving early anyway. They had each other; they didn't exactly need his company. They did need his boat, however, but that wouldn't really be a problem, either. He could leave it here for their use; his truck, too, since it had the trailer hitch for the boat. He could drive back to New Orleans in their car.

Yet what excuse could he give for leaving? The call from his law office? That might work. But then again, it probably wouldn't. Tomorrow was Friday. By the time he got home, it would be the weekend, and Dick wasn't going to buy the story that he had urgent business to conduct then—especially since he'd been out of action and out of the office for several months!

Besides, his conscience would bother him if he just up and left them like that. Both Dick and Janet had been wonderful to him while he'd been in the hospital, as good to him as his own family. Dick had spent many an hour playing chess with him when he could have been off somewhere else enjoying more lively pursuits. Janet had been a gem, too, dropping by every few days to bring him a humorous card, a gag gift, or a plate of home-baked cookies. She'd even run a few errands for him, such as buying his Mother's Day gift and making trips to the bank or the Post Office for him. Just because you were unhappy with your lot, it didn't mean you could just walk away from friends like that, not when you owed them more than you could ever repay. No, he would simply have to tough it out until Sunday afternoon, when he could leave at the same time they did.

Three hours later Marsh and Dick sat in lawn chairs near the picnic table, where Janet and Scotty still remained after their meal. Janet, who hailed originally from Grand Isle, was entertaining Scotty with the story that her family were descendants of the pirate Jean Lafitte, and how one uncle, a bit of a character, had spent most of his life searching for the legendary treasure Lafitte and his men were supposed to have buried. It was precisely the sort of story to excite a young boy, and Scotty avidly hung on to every word.

Marsh smiled with amusement as he listened. Janet knew how to entertain a youngster, that was for sure. It was too bad, he mused, that she and Dick were unable to have a family of their own.

There he went again, he thought in annoyance, thinking too much about children, of marriage, of families. For the most part Dick and Janet seemed content with their life the way it was. If anything, they were proof that people could be happy without having children.

Yes, a niggling thought said quietly, *but then, they have each other and their love. What do you have?*

Marsh was relieved when Janet got up to carry the leftover food and dishes inside the cabin. He jumped up to help, eager for action, any action, that would take him out of his brooding thoughts.

By the time they were finished cleaning up, Marsh found that Scotty had fallen asleep on the sofa.

"Poor little tyke, he's had a long, busy day," Janet said softly.

"That he has," Marsh agreed. "I'd better take him home." He bent over and lifted the sleeping child into his arms. Scotty stirred, but didn't waken. Marsh cradled the boy's head against his shoulder while Dick held open the door. "See you tomorrow," he said in a low voice so that he wouldn't wake the boy.

"Good night," Janet and Dick both whispered. Janet stepped close and dropped a kiss to Scotty's brow before Marsh carried him out into the soft, warm night.

When Pam opened her door to the soft knock and saw Marsh standing there with a tender expression on his face as he gazed down at Scotty's sleeping face, her throat squeezed tight and, for a time, she couldn't speak.

Marsh lifted his head to look at her. "We've got a tired little man here," he said softly, stepping into the room.

Pam led the way to Scotty's bedroom, where she switched on a lamp and then pulled back the bedcovers.

Marsh placed Scotty on the bed and began to remove his tennis shoes while Pam half-lifted the upper portion of his body so that she could remove his shirt. A moment later the jeans were tossed aside as well, and she tucked the covers around him before bending to kiss his cheek.

She moved quietly toward the lamp, about to flick it off, when Marsh surprised her by stooping over the inert form in the bed and planting a kiss of his own on Scotty's brow. Then he stepped back and cleared his throat before turning and walking out of the room.

Pam followed, touched deeply by Marsh's actions. Except for Uncle Bob and Gus, no man had ever genuinely cared about her son until now. Until Marsh. She wanted to thank him, but the words stuck in her throat. She didn't know how to begin to express the feelings that were bursting in her heart.

Softly, she closed the door to Scotty's bedroom, and when she reached the living room she saw that Marsh had paused beside the desk near the door. The desk lamp focused brightly on the books that lay open, and papers were scattered everywhere.

"Looks like you're working pretty late hours," Marsh commented.

Pam sighed wearily and nodded.

"All work and no play makes Jill a dull girl, you know."

Pam ran her hand through her hair before adjusting the collar on her robe in an absent gesture. "I know. You've told me that before. But if I don't come up with the right figures somehow, Jill is likely to go hungry."

"How is that possible?" Marsh asked in surprise. "The place is packed. Aren't you making a profit?"

"I wish." Pam gnawed at her lower lip. "I'm still paying off some debts my uncle incurred, and it's eating an enormous hole into what this place brings in. That's why things are looking a little seedy. All of the cabins need new foundations and a couple of them need new roofs. There are a lot of other things that need to be done, too, that I simply can't afford. I could really use another employee to help Gus with the maintenance, but I can't afford to hire anyone. As it is, tonight I've come to the conclusion that I have no choice but to go further into debt by trying to get a new bank loan. I've put it off as long as I can, so tomorrow I'm driving into Natchitoches to see about it." She sighed again and smiled wryly. "I just hope I won't soon be filing for bankruptcy. If I do, I'm going to need a good attorney. Are you interested in the job?"

Marsh smiled at her lame joke, but the smile did not reach his eyes as he shook his head. "It's not my type of case. You'd better talk to Dick about that. It's right up his alley. But surely you're exaggerating, aren't you, Pam? It's not really that bad, is it?"

"Perhaps not. Yet, anyway. But I am thinking seriously that I may have to put the place up for sale. I'm hoping it won't ever come to that, but it might if I don't get the financing I need."

"I hope not, either," Marsh said softly. There was

the ring of unmistakable sincerity in his voice. "Well," he said abruptly in an entirely different tone. "It's late. I'd better be shoving off."

Pam didn't want him to go. She had a sudden, desperate urge to throw caution to the wind, to fling herself into his arms, to beg his forgiveness, to plead with him not to leave her. A thousand words swirled in her mind, urgent and confusing.

Marsh turned toward the door, and the movement galvanized her into action. She ran across the room and touched his arm, her eyes beseeching as she looked up at him.

"Marsh, please . . ." she began hoarsely. "I hate this . . . this estrangement, this coldness. Can't we be friends, still be . . ." Something in his eyes made her break off.

"Be friends and lovers?" Marsh asked bluntly.

Pam swallowed hard and nodded. Her eyes were large and luminous, speaking her feelings with eloquent silence.

Marsh slowly shook his head and, with his right hand, removed her left hand from his arm, not roughly, not unkindly, yet in a stark gesture of finality. There was a thickness to his voice that hadn't been there earlier when he finally spoke. "I'm sorry. I've made my feelings as plain to you as I know how, Pam. I'm in love with you and I want to build a life with you. I have friends and I've had my share of lovers. It just isn't enough anymore . . . at least, not from you. Maybe . . ." He brushed his hand across his face and looked away. "Maybe what I want from you is unreasonable. I don't know. But if it is, what you want from me is equally unreasonable. I'm through playing games. Between us, it's got to be all or nothing. That's just how it is."

He looked back at her and gazed solemnly at her for a moment longer. He displayed no anger, no hostility, and to Pam that made it all the worse. His eyes were filled with an unspeakable sadness that made her heart weep silently. She knew she was the cause of it.

"Good night, Pam," he said softly. He opened the door and quietly let himself out.

Pam lifted a trembling hand to her lips, and her eyes blurred with tears of regret as the door shut behind him.

"Good bye, love," she whispered. It would have been futile to go after him. Nothing remained to be said.

Chapter Eight

$\mathscr{P}$am was oblivious to the admiring glances that came her way as she sat alone at a restaurant table, absently stirring coffee in which she'd forgotten to add sugar, while she waited for Gus. This morning she had taken extra pains with her appearance. She wore her most becoming tailored outfit, a peach-colored linen suit with a golden-brown silk blouse that lent a refined, understated elegance to her slender frame. Her dark hair was curled and loosely waved around her face, a face that had gone wan and pale with anxiety beneath her makeup.

Pam and Gus had driven into Natchitoches together this morning, and, after dropping her off at the bank, Gus had gone to run a few errands. They needed a new part for the tractor mower and he was also going to the printers to pick up a new batch of brochures and business stationery Pam had ordered.

"Would you like more coffee, ma'am?"

With a start, Pam realized she'd never even taken a sip from the cup on the table before her. "No, thank you," she said politely.

The waitress nodded with a pleasant smile and moved away to the next table.

Pam lifted her cup to her lips, took a sip of the bitter, unsweetened brew, and pulled a face. She set it down again and spooned sugar into it. She was glad Gus wasn't here yet. She needed time to get her emotions under control. Telling him was going to be the hardest thing she had ever had to do.

Maybe she should have ordered a drink from the bar, she thought grimly. Or half a dozen drinks. But she doubted that even an excess of alcohol could blur her ache of despair.

The bank had turned down her request for a new loan. The man who had talked with her, Mr. Landry, had made sympathetic murmurings, but that didn't alter the end result. After two hours of pouring over her financial records, he'd said that with the debt she still owed them, as well as her monthly operating expenses, it simply wasn't prudent to allow her to extend herself still further. "I can see that you're a very responsible person," he'd said kindly, "and it's admirable that you've managed to keep up with your obligations as well as you've done, but if we tacked yet another loan on top of the debts you've already got, you'd go under within six months. My suggestion is that you either take on a partner who has money to invest or put the place up for sale."

"And do you also know anyone interested in becoming a partner in a fishing resort?" she'd asked bitterly. "Or someone who'd like to buy the place outright?"

"I'm afraid not, right offhand," Mr. Landry had replied seriously. "It might take a few months to find the right party, but you'll be able to hold on for a while yet."

Yes, she supposed she could hold on for a while longer. She was in the middle of the busiest season of the year, when the most money was coming in. But what would happen by the dead of winter, when business was at its lowest ebb?

Pam thought it highly unlikely that she could find a partner. Most of the owners of the other nearby fishing resorts she was familiar with were either married couples running a mom-and-pop operation or men. It wasn't realistic to think that she'd actually find a male partner who would share an equal partnership with a woman. So that left selling the place or eventually losing it through bankruptcy.

It wasn't herself she was most concerned about in the matter. She could easily find another teaching position, if not in Many, then somewhere else. But that would be hard on Scotty, uprooting him, moving him to a new town, a new school, new friends. He was so used to having the freedom of acres to run and play in, that confinement in a city apartment would be a hard adjustment for him to make. Still, if it was necessary, it could be done. There were far worse things than that in life.

A more serious concern was what would happen to Gus and Zelma. They'd been working at the resort for many years and they were counting on their pension plan that Uncle Bob had set up for them. Pam had been careful to scrupulously match the money they'd contributed, and it was in an account separate from her routine business account. She'd always been afraid if she ever touched it, borrowed from it, and mixed it in with the general operating funds, that she might not be able to replace it, and that, in her book, would be tantamount to stealing. But, and this was the major question, if the resort was sold, would the new owners be so generous? Would they keep the Emerys on until time for retirement and give them their full pension benefits? Or would they pull the rug out from under them? There was no way of knowing. Certainly, if a bankruptcy occurred, the money in that account would have to be used to help settle up bills, and again the Emerys would be left out in the cold.

Pam ached at the thought and felt suddenly ancient under the heavy weight of her burden. *Oh, Uncle Bob,* she cried silently, *I'm letting you down, even though I've done the best I could.* And that made the pain even more unbearable. The resort had been his whole life, his wife and children and everything else rolled into one. He had put his heart and soul into it, and it was painful to think the place might end up in strangers' hands.

Even so, Pam knew that, had he lived, it was Uncle Bob who would be facing these same problems, simply because he'd overextended himself. Four years ago she had done her best to talk him out of buying those extra ten acres they hadn't really needed and putting in the swimming pool. Now she was merely seeing the results of what he had started.

She looked up to see Gus weaving his way between tables, coming to join her. Her eyes softened as she watched him. She really loved him, and she hated herself for what she had to tell him. Yet there was no way out.

Gus looked a little pale, and when they had ordered lunch, all he asked for was a bowl of soup. Pam looked at him questioningly, because this was so unlike him. "What's wrong?" she asked with concern. "Are you sick?"

Gus shook his head. "No, no, don't worry about me. Just a touch of indigestion this morning, that's all. Probably that sausage I ate for breakfast. I got the part we needed for the mower and picked up the things you wanted at the printers. How'd your business go at the bank?"

Pam lowered her gaze to the table and toyed with a spoon. "I was trying to get a new loan, but they turned me down," she said quietly. "They said we'd go under if we took on more debts." Her voice shook as she added, "The loan officer suggested I try to sell the place, Gus."

To her vast relief, Gus seemed to take the news stoically. "I'm not surprised," he said. "Zelma and I've been aware of what a burden you've been carrying, and it's been a big load. I know you feel bad, like you're letting Bob down by having to sell his place, but you can't look at it that way, Pam. I know you love the place, too, but you have to look after yourself and Scotty's welfare first. If you sell it, the money'll give you a big cushion against the future. At least you wouldn't have to worry about where Scotty's college money will come from."

"I'm more worried about your pension," Pam said frankly. "What if the new owners won't keep you on until retirement?"

Gus grimaced. "It's a possibility," he admitted. "After all, what new owner would want to take on two older employees and the expense of their pension right off the bat? It'll make a hardship for us, all right, no doubt about it, but that's not your problem, honey."

"Yes, it is!" she cried. "It's not fair, and I can't let that happen to you!"

Gus reached across the table and touched her hand with his callused one. "You have to do what you have to do, regardless of personal feelings. Zelma and I love you, and you know that's not going to change, no matter what happens." He shrugged. "If you lose the place, we won't be any better off that way, either. Besides, we won't starve, so stop worrying. We've got a bit tucked away, and I can always sell off that piece of land I have. Did I tell you that Marsh has been thinking about buying it?"

Pam's eyes widened in surprise. "No," she said softly. "I didn't know. Why would he want it?"

"Hmmmph." Gus looked at her sternly. "I had a notion you might know the answer to that better than I would."

"What do you mean?"

"Well," Gus said with pointed emphasis, "it's a

beautiful piece of land. It would make a nice homesite for a young family."

Pam lowered her gaze to the table. "Gus," she said, feeling sick, "I . . . I'd rather we didn't . . ."

Gus ignored her feeble attempt to squash the subject of Marsh. "I kinda figured the two of you were getting pretty thick there for a while, and any fool can see he's crazy about Scotty. But the last few days a body could run a freezer off the cold way you two treat each other. Do you love him, honey?" he asked with the familiarity of a genuine friend.

Pam sighed and twisted the edge of her paper napkin until it became a tight little furl. "Yes, but there are problems. He's leaving Sunday," she added in a bleak voice.

"Don't you realize by now there are always problems? That's just part of life . . . working through one problem to the next. But it's a whole lot easier if you have someone there to work out the problem *with*," he added meaningfully. "Life is difficult enough without having to go it alone."

Pam's heart told her that what he was saying was right, but her head cautioned her to remember the past. Maybe other women honestly didn't mind being bound and chained by a man as long as they had the questionable security that marriage offered, but she was different. Even loving wasn't enough to overcome the dread and horror she felt at the mere thought of marriage, and she couldn't face it a second time. For her, marriage spelled the end of love and the beginning of oppression.

The waitress brought their meal and Pam looked at it

with distaste. So much unhappiness was pressing down upon her that she almost felt as ill as Gus looked.

He noticed she was merely toying with her food and said with false heartiness, "Hey, cheer up! Nobody died, you know. Things have a way of ironing themselves out. Now, eat your lunch like a good little girl."

Pam didn't know whether he had been referring to her business problems or her personal one, but either way she didn't feel very hopeful just now. The grim seriousness of it all had destroyed her appetite, and she had to force herself to swallow even a few bites. Gus, she saw, wasn't eating very much either.

They finally gave up the pretense of eating, paid the check, and went outside into the blazing hot midday sun. Shimmering waves of steam rose from the asphalt pavement of the parking lot as they made their way toward the car. No breeze stirred, so that the heat clung to one's body, cloying, suffocating, brutally intense.

Gus unlocked the car. "Lord, but it's hot today," he said as Pam slid inside, beneath the wheel and over to the passenger side.

"I know." Pam brushed her fingers across her moist forehead and then leaned forward to remove the jacket to her suit. "I'm wilting in this jack—"

A moan unlike any human sound she'd ever heard before riveted her attention. Pam's hands froze on the lapels of her jacket as her head jerked sideways to look toward the direction of the sound. Gus stood before the open car door, his face strangely gray and his hands clutching wildly at his chest.

He moaned again and slumped to the pavement while Pam stared in horrified disbelief.

"Must be a slow day if you've got time to do that," Marsh said. He lifted the soft-drink can to his lips and took a long swallow.

Zelma nodded. Sitting in a chair behind the store counter, she was busily crocheting. "Guess most everybody's still out on the water yet," she said. "It's been kind of slow in here all day."

"What're you making?" Marsh asked idly.

"It'll be a bedspread for Pam when I'm finished," she replied. She held up a few completed white squares to show him. "I plan to give it to her for Christmas."

"It's beautiful. I'm sure she'll love it."

Zelma grinned. "I think so. She's seen me working on it, and commented how much she liked it. She thinks I'm making it for my sister."

"Did Pam go into Natchitoches today?" Marsh asked.

Zelma nodded again, never missing a stitch. "Gus went with her. He had a few things to do too. Trips to town seem to wear him out so much these days," she said with a hint of worry to her voice. "I hope he doesn't come back too tired." She glanced up briefly at Marsh and changed the subject. "What're you doing wasting time hanging around in here? Where are your friends this afternoon?"

Marsh shrugged. "Resting. Almost a week's worth of fishing has just about done them in. I think they'll be ready to head back home on Sunday."

"And you?" Zelma looked up at him shrewdly. "Will you be ready too?"

A distant look came into Marsh's eyes. "More than ready," he said tonelessly. "The only reason I stayed this week was that Janet and Dick were here."

Zelma tilted her head and looked up at him. "And here I'd been hoping all along there was another reason."

They gazed at each other without pretense. Marsh pressed his lips together. "Yeah," he said slowly. "I hoped so too, for a while. But it just didn't work out."

"Maybe if you'll give it more time," Zelma said. "Pam's a little gun-shy when it comes to men. Her marriage was pretty bad."

"I've got a lousy marriage behind me too." Marsh shook his head. "The lady just doesn't want me, Zelma, so if I hung around hoping she'd change her mind, I'd just be wasting my time, and hers too."

"I don't believe that," Zelma protested. "If you want to know what I think, I . . ."

Whatever she thought was to remain forever left unsaid. The telephone rang, breaking off her train of thought. Marsh moved swiftly toward the end of the counter, where the telephone hung on the wall. Holding out a restraining hand toward the older woman, who had her lap full of her crochet materials, he said, "Don't get up. I'll grab it."

"Thanks." Unperturbed, Zelma, who had half-risen while trying to keep from dropping her ball of thread, crocheted square, and needles, sank down again and picked up her work where she'd left off.

"Nye's Resort and Marina," Marsh said into the receiver. "Franklin speaking."

"Marsh?" A shaky voice asked. "Oh, thank God it's you, Marsh!"

Marsh had been lounging in a relaxed fashion against the counter. Something in the tone of her voice made him straighten up, and, with a gut-level instinct, he turned his back to the woman in the store and stared out the plate-glass window.

"Yes, Pam," he murmured softly. "It's me. Are you all right?"

"I don't know. I . . . yes, of course. It . . . oh, Marsh"—her voice rose an hysterical decibel—"Marsh, it's G–G–Gus!" Her words became garbled.

"What?" Marsh strained to hear her. With restraint, he kept his own voice low. "I can't understand you. Now take a deep breath and tell me what's happened."

He heard Pam suck in a ragged breath. After a fraction of a minute, her voice still trembled but was clear enough to be understood. "I'm at the hospital. Here in Natchitoches. Gus . . . Gus has had . . . a heart attack!"

Marsh felt himself stiffen, and he became even more acutely conscious of the woman behind him, only a few feet away, the person who would be most affected by this piece of news. "How bad . . ." He broke off and, carefully schooling his voice and words, changed it to, "How are things?"

"Zelma's right there, isn't she?" Pam asked swiftly.

"Yes."

"All right." She sucked in a second, more rapidly

indrawn breath, and this time her voice was steady, the words precise and businesslike, as though it were the only possible way to state the bad news. "It's bad, Marsh. Zelma should get here as quickly as possible. It happened about an hour ago just as we were leaving a restaurant after lunch. Will you tell her, or do you think I should do it?"

"Perhaps it would be better if I did," Marsh said softly.

"Yes. Yes, you're right. You're there with her and . . . and . . ."

"Exactly. I'll take care of it," he said crisply. He had heard a suspicion of rising hysteria coming on again.

"Tell her to come, Marsh," Pam pleaded unnecessarily.

"Of course. I'll see you shortly," Marsh said in a quiet, calm tone he hoped would help her pull herself together. It was too bad they couldn't speak more freely. "'Bye."

As he hung up the receiver, he drew in a silent, deep breath of his own. He hated like hell to have to turn around and face the woman behind him. Five minutes ago she was talking Christmas presents. Now this. *Why,* he asked himself grimly, *was life so hard?*

"Who was that?" Zelma lifted her eyes from her crochet work as Marsh turned toward her, and, at the somber expression on his face, her hands stilled.

Marsh went around the counter and gathered her time-wrinkled hands in his as he knelt beside the chair. "That was Pam," he said gently. "Gus is in the hospital. They say he's had a heart attack."

"Oh, my . . . oh, dear!" Zelma's hands began to tremble violently. Her crochet supplies tumbled unheeded to the floor as she started to rise, then sank weakly. Her lips quivered, and moisture gathered in the corners of her eyes. "It can't be," she moaned softly. "It can't be."

Marsh's hands tightened around hers, which had suddenly turned cold. "You must think very positive," he said firmly. "Zelma, are you listening to me?" At her stunned nod, he went on, "I want you to sit right here and rest while I fetch Dick to mind the store and watch after Scotty. Then I'm going to drive you to the hospital. To Gus."

Zelma bobbed her head once more, like a sorrowful puppet. Marsh rose and hurried toward the door, anxious about leaving her even for a few minutes. She was in shock, and he wasn't sure what she might do.

Fortunately he spotted Scotty riding down the road on his bike. Quickly, with the little trick he'd learned as a child, Marsh inserted two fingers into his mouth and whistled. The shrill sound was loud and piercing.

At once, Scotty turned in his direction. Marsh motioned for him to come, and obediently the boy whipped the bike around and headed toward him.

Marsh stepped down to the graveled driveway. "Go get Dick and Janet and tell them to come to the store right away. It's very important."

Scotty looked at him searchingly. "What . . . ?"

"I'll explain when you get back. Run quickly, son."

Without a word, Scotty turned his bike and set off, peddling at a furious pace. Marsh went back inside the store to the stunned woman who still sat where he'd left her.

Three more cabins remained to be cleaned. Pam carried her bundle of soiled linen from the cabin she'd just finished cleaning and placed it in the bin in the back of the van before she paused to brush her arm across her moist forehead. Her back ached; in fact, her whole body ached from exhaustion. She wondered wearily whether she would ever feel rested again.

She glanced at her watch. Almost eleven. Time to return to the store to relieve Marsh so that he could be free to repair the stove in cabin two. Pam prayed he could. The last thing she needed now was to have to buy a new one.

At least, she thought as she climbed into the van, she didn't have Scotty to worry about in addition to the multitude of other things she had to do. Yesterday he'd gone to Monroe with Jimmy and his parents to spend a few days at Jimmy's grandmother's house. The timing for such a trip couldn't have been better, and Pam was grateful it had come his way. Like the rest of them, he'd been terrified over Gus and that was a heavy trip for a seven-and-a-half-year-old boy, especially since he wasn't old enough to be allowed visits at the hospital. A few days away was just what he needed to keep him occupied and his mind off his fears.

No such luck for her, however. Her own fears over Gus were ever-present, just beneath the surface of her carefully maintained exterior calm. Whenever she looked at his grayish-white face against the stark white hospital pillow, she felt the dull, heavy weight of guilt; when she looked into Zelma's pale, worried face she found it difficult to speak because of the seemingly permanent lump that was lodged in her throat. When she looked at Marsh, who so quietly and efficiently had assumed many of the numerous duties at the resort, she wanted to cry out in anguished protest. But in front of everyone she kept an outward illusion of stability. By day she worked from dawn till dusk, scarcely stopping to breathe, much less eat; by night she drove the long miles to the hospital to see Gus and Zelma, who maintained a vigil beside her husband. But deep in her secret heart, she wondered how much longer this could go on. For any of them. It had already been two weeks.

Marsh was busy with a customer when she entered the store, and didn't acknowledge her presence. "That'll be two dollars and thirty-four cents," he told the woman at the counter.

Pam made her way behind the counter as the woman paid Marsh, picked up her purchase, and left. Marsh dropped the money into the cash register and the coins made a jingling sound when he closed the drawer. He turned to look at Pam for the first time.

"You look awful," he said with cruel honesty.

Pam lifted her haunted eyes to his face. "Thanks," she said listlessly. "I needed that. Not that you look a whole lot better," she added in a thoughtful voice as she noted the lines of fatigue carving deepening crevices along his forehead and around the edges of his mouth.

Marsh smiled grimly. *"Touché.* I've thought it over,

Pam, and we absolutely have to get some extra help out here. Neither one of us can keep up this pace indefinitely."

Pam stiffened. "You . . . you don't have to, you know," she said in a choked voice.

"Don't I?" His eyes darkened and were penetrating as they studied her face. He stepped toward her and, without warning to either of them that he was about to do it, he pulled her into his arms and pressed her head against his chest.

The unexpected action broke open a dam inside of Pam. She burst into tears.

Marsh's arms tightened their hold and they stood together for a long time. He made no effort to stop her, but merely held her, letting her spill it out of her system. There was no other sound except her muffled sobs against his chest.

After a long time, the sobs became less intense, the shuddering decreased, and Pam grew calmer. Only her eyes continued to tear, wetting Marsh's shirt further because, though she lifted a hand and tried to dash them away, fresh ones kept falling. It was the first time she had cried, really cried, since Gus's heart attack.

Gradually she became aware that Marsh was stroking her hair and was murmuring soothing nothings to her. "I . . . I'm sorry," she whispered. She tried to pull away, but Marsh refused to let her go.

"It's okay," he said quietly. "You had to get it out sometime. You've been under a tremendous strain. Feel better now?"

This time when she tried to pull away, he allowed it, and she managed what she hoped was a reassuring smile. "I'm fine." But she wasn't, really. She was horribly embarrassed about what had just happened. She'd also grown increasingly aware of Marsh himself, of how heavenly it felt to be held in his arms again, to hear the tenor of his low, caressing voice. Because she didn't have the nerve to meet his eyes, she gazed down at the wet spot on his dark blue shirt. "You . . . you'd better go change your shirt," she said prosaically.

"It'll dry," he responded without concern. Marsh put a hand beneath her chin, forcing it upward so that she had no choice but to meet his gaze. Soft color crept into her cheeks and his gray eyes widened in surprise and knowledge. "You're not embarrassed about what just happened, are you?" he asked incredulously.

"Of course I am," she said irritably. She jerked away from him and turned her back so that she wouldn't have to look at him anymore. Emotion shook her voice as she fought the persistent tears. "I'm used to standing on my own two feet," she declared, "not turning into a weeping sob-sister who needs a broad shoulder to cry on. I should be running this place alone, not depending on a generous guest to pitch in and help me out in a crisis. I should have been a better manager in the first place, so that the crisis never happened at all! Oh, damn it," she cried in wild frustration as the latest supply of tears spilled down her cheeks. She lifted both her hands and buried her face in them.

Marsh came behind her and touched her shoulder lightly with one hand. Pam turned on him like a wildwoman, doubling her fists and slamming them against the unyielding hardness of his chest. "Leave me alone!" she yelled. "Just go away and leave me alone!"

The sobbing wracked her body, doubling it over with pain.

Marsh's arm went around her waist and then he was turning her, guiding her around the counter and out of the store. When they got outside into the bright sunlight, he released her for a minute, but Pam was scarcely aware of anything, not why she was out here, not where she was going, nor even what he was doing. Her entire world had crumbled, and now her body seemed to be crumbling too.

Again Marsh's arm came around her, and he guided her toward his truck and helped her inside. Weak now, beyond questioning, beyond decision-making, she allowed him to lead. Once she was settled, he closed the door, went around to the driver's side, and got behind the wheel.

Marsh drove to his cabin and stopped. "I'll only be a minute. Wait here," he told her. Pam was only dimly aware of his getting out of the truck and going inside. She didn't care. At the moment nothing mattered except this tremendous storm that was going on inside her mind and body.

When Marsh returned, he carried a small ice chest and a blanket. He stowed both in the back of the truck before getting inside with Pam.

By now she was once again becoming calm. She felt thoroughly exhausted, drained, but in a strange way she felt better. Inside, she had been washed clean. Her mind had cleared.

"Where are we going?" she asked quietly.

Marsh glanced at her as he started the ignition. "On a picnic."

Pam shook her head. "We can't. There's no one at the store."

"The world can survive a couple of hours without the store. You need a break. I need a break. Therefore," he added sternly, but with a softness in his eyes, "we are going on a picnic. Now," he looked at her quizzically, "would you like to go inside and wash your face before we go?"

"I think I'd better," she said shakily. "I must look a real sight."

Marsh leaned across the seat and brushed her lips with his, so lightly that she could almost think she had imagined it. "A sight," he agreed. "And very real, too." He brushed a finger beneath her eye, wiping away the dampness there. "Real tears, real lips, real emotions. Real flesh and blood." He gave his head a tiny shake. "What is it about you?" he asked rhetorically. "Every time I think I've figured you out, I find new facets to you." He smiled and gave her a gentle push. "Now, hurry up and wash your face. I'm hungry."

For their picnic, Marsh took her to Gus's land where they'd camped out with the boys. They got out of the truck and, carrying the small ice chest and blanket, Marsh led the way through a thick, shady stand of pine trees. The air smelled sweet and clean, heavy with the scent of pine, and their footsteps were cushioned by the ground spread of fallen needles.

When they emerged from the trees into the sunlight, the wide, glittering expanse of the reservoir burst into view. Far out on the blue water a lone fishing boat could be seen. This area, on both sides of the water, was more secluded, more private, a far distance away from the bustle always surrounding commercial fishing camps. It was as though they had the lake and the forest all to themselves, except for the birds that chirped in a nearby tree.

Marsh deposited the ice chest on a level stretch of ground just above a slope that reached toward the water's edge. A cypress tree's sprawling branches and fluttering leaves cast a pleasant shade over the spot.

"Well, what do you think?" Marsh asked.

Pam was looking toward the water, and she nodded her approval and inhaled deeply. "It's a wonderful place for a picnic." She turned to find Marsh watching her and she smiled at him. "Thanks for bringing me. I think I needed this."

"We both did." Marsh held out one corner of the blanket toward her, and together they spread it over the ground.

The combination of fresh air and utter peace of the location gave Pam an appetite she hadn't had in weeks, and she ate the chicken salad sandwiches Marsh had made with ravishing appreciation.

They spoke little while they ate. Afterwards they stowed away the remains of their meal, and, while Marsh stretched out on the blanket, with his arms crossed behind his head, Pam sat beside him, hands clasped around her knees as she gazed at the lake. The serenity of the surroundings was slowly draining away some of the stress she'd been under for the past two weeks. The rippling water mesmerized her, soothing and calming her like a mother does when she strokes a fevered infant's brow.

A half hour went by in total silence, and then Marsh

broke it unexpectedly by asking, "What are you thinking?"

Pam glanced down at him. He had shifted onto his side, his head propped up by one hand as his elbow pressed into the blanket. The shadows made his hair seem almost midnight black, and his eyes were all but concealed, both by the deep shade and his heavily drooping eyelids, but a shaft of light, penetrating through the foliage, painted bright highlights on the rest of his face. She found herself suddenly fascinated by the full sensuality of his lips.

She looked away again, toward the water. "I thought you'd fallen asleep," she said quietly. She shrugged her shoulders. "I was just thinking how I wished life could be simple and uncomplicated and happy."

"Can't it be?"

She shook her head. "I don't know. If it can, it's escaped me completely thus far."

Marsh levered himself upward into a sitting position beside her, and his gaze, too, scanned the water. "Maybe that's more an attitude, a belief system, than anything else," he said thoughtfully. "Maybe it's something you have to deliberately aim for if you're to ever achieve it."

"Maybe." Pam picked up a browned pine needle and flicked it against one knee. "Maybe it's also a matter of luck." She sighed. "And a lack of guilt."

"Guilt?" Marsh's voice was softly questioning.

"When I was a little girl and my parents fought, I used to feel so guilty. I kept thinking if I was a better person, they'd be happier and wouldn't argue so much. When they divorced, I was devastated and I thought it was my fault that they didn't want to live together anymore. Because I was in the way, I thought they didn't love me. Oh, I know how silly that sounds, but that's how I felt. And then with Mike, I felt if I'd only done something differently, he'd have been happy too . . . with me, with Scotty, even with himself."

"And now?" Marsh asked quietly. Pam could feel his searching gaze upon her. "You still feel guilty now?"

She nodded. "I've let everyone down. Uncle Bob, because I can't hold on to his place much longer and I know it, and I owed him so much. In his own gruff way, he was better to me than anybody else ever was in my entire life. If he hadn't helped me after Mike and I separated, I don't know what would have become of Scotty and me." Her voice grew husky. "And now there's Gus. If I hadn't told him what the banker said that day, if I hadn't told him I'd have to sell the resort and that it would jeopardize both his and Zelma's pensions, he'd never have had that attack. If he dies . . ." She broke off and squeezed her eyes shut.

Marsh put his arms around her and again, weakly, Pam gave into the solace she found there. She dropped her head against his shoulder.

"He isn't going to die," Marsh said firmly. "He's coming along tremendously and you know it. The doctors are very optimistic. Besides, you can't blame yourself like this. Gus hadn't been feeling well for the past couple of months. You heard him say so. The doctors said it could have happened at any time, at any place."

"Yes, but it happened then, with me. After I'd dumped all that bad news on him."

"Blaming yourself is pointless, Pam," Marsh said, sounding slightly impatient. "It's just as ridiculous as blaming yourself for your parents' differences. You can't possibly function by carrying around a load of guilt that's not your burden. I don't know what happened in your marriage, but even if you're partly to blame for its failure, I'm sure your husband earned his share of it, too."

His eyes met hers as he looked down at her, and they fell silent. All the feelings they'd had for each other, that had been held at bay for weeks, now came surging back like a gigantic tidal wave. A poignant longing shook Pam as Marsh's gray eyes seemed to devour her with a hunger he could no longer hide.

Pam's throat was dry and her words came out raspy as she spoke. "I . . . I appreciate your staying on to help me out like you've done, Marsh. More than I can say." She couldn't add that he was a part of her guilt as well—guilt that she'd been leaning on him, guilt that he had stayed on these past two weeks only because she'd desperately needed somebody, guilt because of their submerged passions, because she couldn't give him what he most needed. "I would have gone under completely these past couple of weeks if it hadn't been for you."

"You're welcome," Marsh said simply. "I wanted to do it for you, for Gus and Zelma as well. I couldn't have gone away with things being as they are. Besides," —he smiled and looked away—"I like it here . . . this little corner of heaven. It pulls at me." He broke the almost unbearable intensity of their gaze by looking away toward the trees.

"Gus told me that day at lunch that you were considering buying this land from him," Pam said. "Are you going to?"

Marsh shrugged. "I don't think so. It's a wonderful place for a permanent home or even a weekend place, but there wouldn't be any point in my buying it, because I wouldn't ever use it." His gaze returned to her face and an undeniable tension sprang up between them. "Once I leave here, I won't be coming back, Pam," he said with stark finality.

She lowered her gaze and fought the sickening despair that squeezed her heart. "I know," she said in a small, forlorn voice.

Gently, she lifted her head from his shoulder and tried to withdraw from his arm. But the action incited Marsh, and, swiftly, he jerked her back to him as both arms went around her this time. Something like dark anger burned in his eyes just before his lips, arrogant and firm and ruthless, took possession of hers.

His mood, his touch, his kiss, were strange. Pam sensed his anger and resentment, but she sensed something more as well . . . a depth of unhappiness that matched her own, and a need, a strong, urgent need that was overwhelming him.

For a moment she tried to resist; this was madness, and led to nowhere. Her hands fluttered against his shoulders, trying to push him away, and she attempted to twist her head so that she could break the contact of their lips. But it was impossible. Marsh ignored her efforts as his lips ground into hers, forcing hers open so that he could have access to the sweet dark warmth of her mouth.

Pam tried to school her mind into numbness, so that she wouldn't feel, wouldn't be affected, but of course it was futile. Her limbs went weak as awakening desire overtook her. She couldn't pretend any longer; she ached for him.

The hands that had been fighting ceased their exertions and instead curled around Marsh's neck. The lips that had resisted his bruising kisses softened and yielded.

Marsh felt the change in her and became still. Then, with a gentleness that was all the more noticeable in contrast to his rough manner of a moment before, he pressed her back, lower and lower until her head touched the blanket.

Pam's eyes were closed against the sunlight, against Marsh, against the day itself, and she gave herself up completely to the passionate sensations as his hands caressed her.

He touched her everywhere, her breasts, her hips, her tender inner thighs, and Pam's body came passionately alive, quivering, burning, begging for more. Her own hands were occupied stroking him, running through his hair, teasing the back of his neck, sliding up and down at the curve of his back. Heavy desire muted the lapping sounds of the water, the singing of the birds, the sigh of the breeze through the trees. Everything dimmed and faded except for the insistent, clamoring need within her that built and built ever higher.

Marsh's hand went to her throat and then to the top button on her shirt. But all at once he pulled back from her altogether and groaned, "What are we doing?"

Pam opened her eyes and looked at him in confusion.

"What do you mean? What's wrong?" She sat up and ran a shaky hand through her hair as Marsh got to his feet.

He shook his head and his voice was gruff. "I don't want you like this, Pam."

"Marsh?" Her question was compressed into that single word.

"I want you so badly I think I could die from the wanting, but not like this, a snatched brief hour and still the parting ahead."

"It . . . it doesn't have to be like that," she said huskily.

"No?" His tone was harsh now, filled with anger. "Then what are you offering? An affair whenever I'll have the time to come visit on the occasional weekend? Slipping away from Scotty and coming to a secluded rendezvous like this? A string of motel rooms?"

"You're making it sound so sordid!" she cried hotly. "And it isn't! I love you."

His laugh was taunting. "Sure you do. But it's just not the sort I want." He whirled around and stared across the waters for a long time, and when he spoke again at last, his tone was flat, almost lifeless. "Last night Gus told me the doctors think he can come home next week. I'll stay and help you out until then, when Zelma can come back to work. If it turns out she can't, you'll just have to hire someone else. I need to get back to my own life. It's been on hold long enough."

Chapter Nine

On the evening of the day Gus returned home, Marsh, Pam and Scotty went to visit him for a short, quiet celebration. Just the fact that he was home again seemed to do wonders for him, Pam thought; his color was better than it had been even two days before, when she'd last seen him, and his spirits were high. He joked about Zelma turning into a jack-in-the-box trying to do things for him before he could even think about wanting them, and that if he didn't watch it, instead of the old ticker getting him, she would kill him with kindness.

"What's it like being in a hospital?" Scotty asked as he cuddled next to Gus in the big recliner chair in the Emerys' living room.

"About like being in prison, I reckon," Gus told him. "This one nurse was like a big dragon with a witch's face and she was always ordering me around, telling me to do this or don't do that. I'll tell you, Scotty, if I'd had the energy I'd have hauled her down here to the lake and thrown her in!"

Scotty giggled. "Did she have a big crooked nose like a witch?" he asked.

"You bet. And a bigger mouth. Boy, she was a bossy one. Almost bossier than Zelma."

Scotty giggled again as Zelma made a face. "Now you know good and well, Gus Emery," she scolded, "that if the nurses and I've been bossy, it was only for your own good." Her face softened, losing its mock sternness. "And it sure is good," she added, "to see you sitting in that chair again."

"Amen to that," Pam said huskily.

"I'll bet the doctors have ordered you to get out and do a lot of walking, haven't they?" Marsh asked.

"Yup. First thing you know I'll be up to jogging, and then I'll have a race with Scotty."

Zelma brought out coffee and a cake she'd baked the night before after she'd known for sure Gus would be coming home. They talked about how busy the resort had been and told Gus about the young man Pam had hired at Marsh's adamant insistence to take on the heavy maintenance work around the resort.

"But you needn't feel you've been replaced," Pam hastened to assure him. "There'll still be plenty of work for you to do when you come back. You can help out more in the store, for one thing."

Gus grimaced. "I hate indoor work. I'll do it for a while, but only until I get back on my feet for good."

No one argued with him, and Marsh adroitly changed the subject.

Pam fell silent while the others talked, not daring to bring up the subject that was paramount in her thoughts. It was too soon, and nothing was firm yet.

During the afternoon the most astounding thing had happened. The loan officer from the bank in Natchitoches, Mr. Landry, had called to say that he just might have found her that interested buyer for the resort, depending on her asking price, of course. He had been called this morning by a man wondering if he knew of a business such as hers that was for sale. When he mentioned her resort, the man said he was familiar with it, had stayed at it himself, and that it was exactly the sort of place he wanted. Even more astounding, he told the bank officer that if he bought it, he would like to keep on all the employees, including Pam as manager.

Mr. Landry had asked for her lawyer's name and promised to get in touch with him at once, since the potential buyer chose to have his lawyer negotiate through hers. Pam was still in something of a state of shock over this sudden turn of affairs, and she wasn't sure whether she was elated or sad. Mostly, she just felt numb. If the sale went through, it would solve a multitude of problems . . . a job for her, keeping the same home for Scotty, preserving Gus and Zelma's jobs, too, as well as their pensions. It all sounded too good to be true. But she felt a deep regret at the thought of giving up ownership of the place. It was the only thing she had ever really owned in her life.

But then again, it really hadn't been hers. It had been Uncle Bob's, and he had merely left it in her keeping.

"More coffee, Pam?" Zelma asked.

Pam came out of her foggy thoughts and shook her head. "No, thanks. I won't sleep tonight if I do." Not that she'd been sleeping much any night lately.

She felt Marsh's gaze on her, and, when she looked at him, irresistibly drawn, unable to stop herself, she saw that he was reading her mind. He knew she wasn't sleeping well, just as he knew why.

"Pam's had a hard day, and she's pretty tired," he said now. "Maybe we ought to be going so she can get a good night's sleep for a change. Besides, we don't want to stay too long and wear out Gus." Marsh got to his feet and smiled down at the older man. "It's great to see you home again and looking so well, Gus. You just take it easy, will you, and not try to rush things?"

Gus grinned. "That's a promise," he said fervently. "I'm in no hurry to rush off and play with the angels. I gotta stick around and keep Zelma away from all those young guys."

Zelma sniffed. "Unfortunately it's been many a year since you've had to worry about the competition."

The two of them shared an amused smile, a fond smile, an intimate, secret smile that bespoke an unshakable belief and trust in each other after so many years together.

Pam's throat tightened at the sight, and again she felt Marsh's eyes compelling her to meet his. When she looked at him, this time she could read his thoughts. *You see,* his expression was saying, *love can succeed . . . for a lifetime.*

Maybe, she thought. In some cases. A few special cases. But she already had a history of failure behind her. She wasn't Zelma and Marsh wasn't Gus. She carried scars from her past, and she could never be nineteen again, untouched, naive and innocently hopeful. Perhaps if she had met Marsh first . . . Only she hadn't.

Pam wrenched her gaze from Marsh's and shortly thereafter they had bid their good-byes, Scotty had planted one last kiss on Gus's cheek, and they were outside in the velvety night, climbing into the cab of Marsh's truck.

When they reached the storefront, Pam dug in her purse and pulled out the key to the apartment. "Run on upstairs and unlock the door," she suggested to Scotty. "I'll be along in just a minute."

"Okay. 'Night, Marsh," Scotty said as he slid out of the truck and hopped down to the ground.

"'Night, Scotty." Marsh idly rubbed his forefinger along the steering wheel as he waited for Pam to speak.

After a moment, she said, "Gus . . . Gus looks really well after what he went through, don't you think?" He heard the hope in her voice.

"Yes, he does." He half-turned toward her and their knees accidentally brushed.

Her face was partially concealed by shadows while lights from the storefront cast soft highlights to her cheekbones and lips. She looked somber and deeply thoughtful, and Marsh had to restrain the impulse to reach out to her, to hold her and offer comfort. He could guess what she was feeling.

"I need to go into Natchitoches tomorrow," she said.

"On business. I . . . I know I keep imposing on you, Marsh, but I don't know what else to do. Will you tend the store and watch Scotty while I'm gone?"

"Of course," he said softly. "You didn't really need to ask, you know."

She looked at him, her lips tremulous, her eyes suddenly bright as they caught the reflection of the store lights. "Why are you so good to me?" she asked huskily. "Why do you keep helping me in spite of everything?"

Marsh's lips compressed together. "Maybe I'm a fool," he said, more to himself than to her.

While Pam was away the next day, he thought about that again. Was he being a fool? he wondered. He'd never before been so giving or tried so hard to help any woman. She appreciated it, he knew, but it hadn't essentially changed anything. He supposed he just kept hoping her armor would crack, that whatever wall she had built up around her heart would come tumbling down and she would see what he saw so clearly, that they needed each other's love and the sustenance they could give to each other.

She was such a puzzle to him; she wanted to be independent, she spoke of marriage as though it were a prison, yet Pam didn't fit the pattern of a dedicated liberationist. She had graciously accepted his help these past few weeks, albeit with embarrassment and chagrin that she'd needed it at all. She was anxious about the state of her business affairs, yet she wasn't driven, with blind or ruthless ambition. She was merely a woman trying to keep her head above water, trying to make a decent life for herself and her son.

She said she loved him and, while there was a time when he hadn't believed that, strangely enough he did now. It was too evident in her eyes whenever she looked at him; whenever they touched, accidentally or deliberately, she was as instantly aflame as he. Yet some dark secret deep inside her had her terrified of marriage itself. Whatever had gone on during that time she had been married to Scotty's father, it had turned her off the institution for good. Marsh wished he knew what it was, but though she had let small hints drop occasionally, Pam had never really talked to him about it.

How could he possibly fight an enemy when he couldn't even identify it? At first he'd thought the opponent was the loving memory of her husband, but later he'd realized it wasn't a past love he had to overcome, but her fears that whatever her first marriage had been like, would be again. She had these crazy guilt hang-ups that included the failure of her marriage, and Marsh was beginning to think no one could ever overcome them.

It was shortly after one o'clock that afternoon when Pam returned. She came into the store, lovely in a sky-blue summer dress with sandal heels. Her hair was slightly ruffled from the breeze and, to Marsh, that only added to her attraction.

"Hi," he said quickly in an offhanded manner calculated to conceal his reaction just at seeing her walk through the door looking so cool and beautiful. "Big news. While you were away I booked three cabins for the next two weeks and five trailer sites. Plus I've had a booming business in soft drinks and ice this afternoon, although that *could* be a result of the hot weather more than from my super-salesmanship." He won a smile from her for his efforts and, heartened, he asked as though it were an afterthought, "Did you get your business accomplished?"

Pam nodded and dropped her white clutch purse onto the counter. "I've got big news, too, Marsh!" she told him. Excitement laced her voice.

"Hmmmm." Marsh watched her closely beneath half-closed eyes. "What happened? Somebody leave you a fortune?"

Pam laughed, and Marsh was pleased at the sound. It wasn't often he heard her do that, which was a pity because it was such a sweet, lilting sound. "Not exactly, but you're close," she said. "I've been to see Uncle Bob's lawyer. Someone wants to buy the resort!"

Marsh's eyes widened, taking note of the heightened color of her cheeks. "No kidding?"

She nodded again. "No kidding. The banker called yesterday to tell me about it, so today I carried my books to the lawyer so that he and the buyer's attorney can go over them together. Once they determine that my accounts are accurate, a down payment will be forthcoming. Oh, Marsh, this will solve so many problems for me!"

"Then I'm happy for you," Marsh said quietly. "If you're happy?"

Some of the excitement faded and her gorgeous blue eyes that never ceased to fascinate him suddenly clouded. "As happy as I can be about having to sell Uncle Bob's place, I suppose," she said somberly.

"It's not what you want? To get out from beneath the burden of it all?"

"Of course it isn't!" she exclaimed. "I never wanted to have to sell, but I don't have any choice." She shrugged. "Anyway, as long as I have to sell, it couldn't be better. The man who wants to buy is offering an excellent price. He needs a place like this for investment and tax purposes, I understand. But what makes it ideal is that he's willing to keep on Gus and Zelma and me as well!"

The soft blue eyes were bright again. Marsh smiled at her. "Then nothing really has to change, does it?" he asked quietly.

Pam shook her head. "Only that I won't be the owner anymore. But maybe it's best that way, sad as it makes me feel. This is such a beautiful piece of land, and the resort should be kept in first-rate condition. I've hated to see it so run down, and yet I was struggling enough just to keep abreast of the most urgent repairs. This place needs some money thrown into it and apparently the new owner will be able to do that."

Two days later Zelma returned to work for the first time since Gus's illness. Pam was delighted to have her back. It eased the work load enormously. But her return also brought a private unhappiness that Pam kept carefully hidden. Now that Zelma was back and the new young man Marsh had hired for her was working out so well, she knew it was only a matter of time before Marsh himself went away—a very short time.

The sun was still a fiery orange ball in the sky above the lake when Pam closed the store that afternoon. For once she didn't feel so tired at the end of the day as she had been of late, a direct result of having Zelma back, of course.

She walked toward the stairs, about to go up to the apartment, when she heard Rusty's bark followed by Scotty's excited shout.

"Mom, hey Mom!"

Pam turned to see her son flying toward her at a high speed on his bike while Rusty bounded alongside him. Scotty wheeled in beside her, braking just in the nick of time before almost crashing into the stairs. He was dusty—face it, Pam mentally corrected herself—filthy. Particles of sawdust clung to his wild mop of hair and beads of dirt were caked around his neck, elbows, and knees. The bare feet, she decided wryly, might never come clean again, and as for his clothes, they were probably hopeless. She sighed in sympathy for all mothers of little boys everywhere.

"What on earth have you been doing?" she asked while he caught his breath. "Rolling in the dirt all day?"

"No! Me 'n' Marsh have been building my treehouse! Come see it, Mom! It's super!"

"Treehouse?" Pam asked in surprise. "Where did you get the lumber for it?"

"Marsh went to town at noon and bought it. We've been working on it all afternoon." Scotty grinned with pride. "You're gonna like it, Mom. It's big!"

"Is that so? Well, lead the way. Let's take a look at it," she said, manufacturing enthusiasm. She had a heavy feeling of forboding that the treehouse was Marsh's gesture of good-bye to Scotty.

The treehouse was indeed fine, sturdy and large. It had a roof, a wide, hinged door and two smaller hinged window openings. Scotty insisted Pam climb the ladder to peer inside, and she saw that already he'd stored a few of his treasures in it. There was his toy hunting knife, a flashlight, an old army blanket Gus had given him last year, a water canteen, and, she noted with amusement, a box of cookies she recognized as obviously having been snatched from her own kitchen, no doubt to ward off any possibility of starvation.

"It's wonderful," she praised with admiration after she'd climbed down to the ground again. "I hope you thanked Marsh for doing all this for you."

"I did," Scotty assured her. "Honest. Mom, can I go call Jimmy and see if he can come spend the night? I can't wait till he sees my treehouse!"

Pam smiled. "I don't see why not. And then, my friend, how about taking a bath before seeds start sprouting in your ears?"

"Aw, Mom."

Pam grinned at him as he mounted his bike. "I'll be home in a little while to start supper," she told him. "I think I'll walk down to the duck pond first."

"Okay. See ya." Scotty took off again in the only gear he ever used—first—with Rusty leaping along behind him. Dust rose from the road, billowing over both boy and dog, neither of whom it seemed to bother.

Pam set off at a more decorous pace, rounding the bend, then leaving the road to go off at a tangent, skirting the swimming pool where a few parents splashed with their children and crossing the wide green where a volleyball net was set up. A man and woman in their fifties were volleying a ball back and forth to each other.

When she reached the pond, she found the ducks gliding serenely over the placid waters. A frog hopped along the muddy bank, then disappeared into the water. A bumblebee hovered near a clump of bright yellow sunflowers. Here wildlife was undisturbed by the concerns of mankind. The hustle and bustle and intensity of human beings rushing around worrying and creating their own problems and disorders seemed a bit absurd by comparison; nature had its own sense of order and went about its business with quiet conviction, without hysterics or fanfare.

A sense of peace stole over Pam as she sat down on the bench and allowed the surroundings to soothe her. For a time she blotted out the concerns that constantly weighed upon her. If one did the best one could in life, there was little point in berating oneself later if the final choice happened to have been the wrong one. No one held a crystal ball that could pinpoint the future with unerring accuracy. Even so, the aching sadness around her heart didn't lift. She knew she was making the right choices, the only choices, but she still yearned after the fantasy of what she wished could have been.

A knowing, an awareness, came suddenly that she was no longer alone. Pam turned and saw Marsh. He stood silently, a few yards distant, watching her.

Her heart twisted at the sight of him and a dryness came to her throat. She knew what he had come to tell her even before he spoke.

He approached her with a purposeful stride. He wore navy slacks with a navy-and-white pullover shirt, and the deep color seemed to darken his winter-gray eyes. Slashes of sunlight penetrating through the trees cast burnished copper highlights to his hair. Pam thought she had never seen him looking better. He rarely walked with a limp anymore; his leg was healed and only exhibited signs of the injury it had sustained whenever he happened to be extremely tired. The long weeks of his stay in the sun had bronzed his skin, erasing the sickly hospital pallor he'd had when he'd first arrived. Now he looked vibrantly healthy, strong, virile and infinitely appealing.

"You're taking some time for yourself for a change," he said with approval. "That's good. You don't do it nearly often enough."

Pam forced a smile. "There hasn't been much time for pampering myself of late," she reminded him. "Or for you, either. But it doesn't seem to have done you any harm. I was just thinking how wonderful you look. You never even limp anymore."

"I'm fine," Marsh said shortly. "Being outdoors so much has been good for me. I may have worked hard these past few weeks, but I didn't have the mental stress you've been under. Feeling any happier about selling the place now?"

"A little," she replied. "At least I'm coming to terms with it. And I'm really pleased that I don't have to uproot Scotty or search for a new job."

Marsh shrugged. "Kids adapt quickly. If you had been forced to move, it probably would've been easier on him than on you."

"I suppose." In a brighter voice, Pam said, "I just came from seeing the new treehouse. Scotty's so thrilled with it. It was awfully nice of you to do that for him, Marsh."

Marsh flashed a smile that made her feel as though the sun was just coming out. "I enjoyed doing it," he said. "However, I had to do some fast talking to convince him that we really didn't need to christen it tonight by the two of us sleeping in it."

Pam laughed. "So *that's* why he wanted to see if Jimmy could come out to stay the night! Should I allow it, Marsh?" she asked uncertainly. "They're still awfully young to be staying outdoors all alone at night."

"I don't think it'll hurt," he replied seriously. "Since it has walls and doors, they can't possibly fall out, and animals can't climb that high to bother them."

"I guess you're right," Pam said slowly. "It's just so hard sometimes to stop being the protective mother and let go."

"I'd say you're striking a pretty good average," Marsh said. "Scotty's a lucky boy, having you."

"Thanks," she said softly.

Their eyes met for a long, wordless exchange, and Pam's gaze clung to his. Their eyes spoke everything there was to say—their desires . . . and their pain.

For a breathless moment it seemed to her that he might reach out to touch her, to kiss her, but then Marsh broke the paralyzing thread that held them immobile by propping one foot on the edge of the bench and training his eyes on the sheltered, shady pond. "I came," he said quietly, "to tell you that I'll be leaving now that Zelma's back to help you."

Pam nodded and swallowed. "I know," she said with difficulty. Another, longer silence fell between them until finally she asked in a raspy voice, "When?"

"Day after tomorrow. I thought I'd go fishing tomorrow one last time. And tomorrow night Zelma and Gus have invited me to have dinner with them."

"I see." She had an insane urge to fling herself into his arms and beg him not to go. But she didn't dare weaken her resolve. For both their sakes, she had to be strong. Otherwise she would only end up wrecking both their lives.

The following evening Marsh did his best to be entertaining, to enjoy himself, and to a small extent he succeeded.

Zelma had prepared a delicious country-style meal of ham, peas, mashed potatoes, corn on the cob, and fresh-from-the-oven buttermilk biscuits. For dessert, there was blackberry cobbler topped with vanilla ice cream. Marsh ate with a hearty appetite, as did Scotty, who had come with him tonight, and he could see that they greatly pleased Zelma.

"A little more cobbler, Marsh?" she offered when he'd polished off the huge portion she had given him.

"No, thank you, Zelma. I don't know where I'd put another bite. Everything was wonderful, as usual. You really do cook like an angel. If you ever want to leave Gus for that younger man," he joked, "I'll be first in line."

Zelma laughed. "I might as well," she said. "Gus just eats like a bird since he's been home. It's no fun cooking for him anymore."

"Hmmph!" Gus pretended to be disgruntled. "Marsh might want you for your cooking, but he'd soon hand you back, you've turned into such a nag. 'Gus, take your medicine,'" he mimicked. "'Gus, you need to walk and get your exercise. Gus, you need to rest more. Gus, that's too heavy for you to lift.' Lord love her, Marsh," he exclaimed, "she watches every move I make like a hawk. A man can't get any peace when she's around!"

Marsh grinned. "Same old complaint, huh? And how would you feel if she ignored you and didn't give a hoot at all? *Then* your nose would be out of joint for sure."

Gus grinned wryly and they all laughed. "Well, since you put it that way, maybe I can stand her nagging a little longer."

"You'd better, you old grouch," Zelma told him. "I don't know who else is going to put up with your bad temper and ornery ways."

Gus winked at Marsh and decided to soothe ruffled feathers. "I guess it's just your cross to bear, living with me and all my faults."

"I guess it is," Zelma said, grinning at him. "But I've invested so much time on you now, I'd just as soon keep you around a few years longer, faults and all."

As they all left the table, Gus said to Scotty, "You be sure and tell your mom what a good dinner she missed out on by not coming tonight."

"Okay," Scotty replied. "Gus, you've got to get better so you can come see my treehouse. Marsh and I built it together," he boasted proudly.

"Is that a fact?" Gus asked. Together, they moved toward the door to the living room.

Marsh started to help clear the table, but Zelma stopped him. "This is your last night with us and I'd rather you spent it visiting with Gus and Scotty than helping me clean in the kitchen."

His last night. While he sat in the living room talking quietly with Gus and Scotty sprawled on the floor putting together a puzzle Zelma had given him, it seemed almost unreal to Marsh that in only a few more hours he would be leaving here, going back home where he belonged, back to his family and his work. It felt as though he were leaving home instead, and his heart was heavy. During the past two months Gus and Zelma had become like a second family to him, as well as Scotty and Pam.

His gaze fell on the child who lay on his stomach across the floor. The tip of Scotty's tongue jutted between his lips as he concentrated on the puzzle pieces scattered around him. Telling the child earlier today that he was leaving hadn't been easy. Tears had welled up in Scotty's eyes and he had asked with real anguish, "Will you come back, Marsh? Will you come to see me?"

"I'll try," he'd replied, not knowing how else to answer.

By nine-thirty, Scotty had fallen asleep in the middle of the floor despite the voices of the three adults who sat talking nearby. Marsh noticed him first and smiled. "I guess I'd better take him home."

"Never mind," Zelma said. "He can sleep here tonight. Just stop in and tell Pam when you get back. If you'll carry him, Marsh, I'll get the bed ready in the spare room."

A few minutes later Scotty was tucked beneath the covers. In the darkened bedroom, after Zelma had returned to the living room, Marsh stood for a long time gazing at the sleeping child and remembering another night when he'd carried Scotty to bed with Pam at his side. That had been a sweet moment, never to be repeated.

Sighing, Marsh bent and swept Scotty's hair from his brow. He kissed the child's smooth forehead and whispered, "Good-bye, Scotty. I'm really going to miss you."

He went back to join the Emerys and visited with them for another half hour. At ten o'clock he got up to leave, feeling that Gus needed to go to bed himself, but he could tell that both Gus and Zelma genuinely hated saying good-bye, and so did he.

When Marsh got back to the resort, a nighttime hush had fallen over it. The pool was closed, the playground empty, the marina silent and dark, the store locked tight. Only an occasional pole light along the road cast illumination against black trees and inky blue sky, and here and there could be seen a light shining from a trailer window or from behind the curtains of a cabin.

A single light also shone from Pam's living-room window. Marsh parked his truck in the drive and climbed the stairs to knock on the door. His heart felt heavy at the thought that after tonight he wouldn't be seeing her again, at least not for a long while and then not in a way that really counted.

Pam had heard the pickup stop and she hurried at once to answer the door, relieved to abandon the book she'd been trying to kid herself she was reading. The truth was she'd absorbed little of it. Tonight all her thoughts had been on Marsh and the desolation she felt over his leaving.

When she opened the door, her pulse quickened at the imposing sight of him. His face was so precious to her, and she tried to memorize it, knowing this was her last opportunity.

"Hi." She summoned a wan smile. "How was the evening?"

"Fine. They missed you."

"I . . . I had too much to do here," Pam said lamely, knowing they both were aware her excuse was a weak lie.

"Scotty fell asleep and Zelma insisted on putting him to bed. She'll bring him when she comes in the morning."

Pam nodded. "That's all right. Er . . . would you like to come in?" she asked with stiff politeness. She felt so strange. She didn't know how to say good-bye.

She thought he might refuse, but then he nodded his dark head and stepped over the threshold, softly closing the door behind him.

"Well, are you done packing?" she asked with a forced cheerfulness that caused her vocal cords to ache.

"Just about," Marsh said. His own voice was flat, without vitality. "It won't take long to finish in the morning."

"What time are you leaving?"

"Early. I want to be on the road by daylight."

"I . . . see." The words hit her harder than she'd expected, and Pam's lips quivered. "Then I suppose I'd better say good-bye now, hadn't I?" she asked huskily.

She lifted her eyes to his and, like the previous afternoon, they were both suddenly, hopelessly ensnared, unable to articulate words, powerless to look away. Pam felt a deep pain building up inside her, spreading its icy fingers around her heart. Her eyes blurred and her lips trembled. All at once, she simply couldn't bear it.

"Don't go!" she cried out in an anguished voice. "Oh, Marsh, I'll miss you so." Stumbling over the hem of her robe, she rushed toward him, hands outstretched.

Marsh caught her to him and his mouth descended on hers with a fierce, hot urgency. "Oh, God," he groaned raggedly as he covered her face with kisses, "I want you and I can't fight it anymore. I've tried, I've really tried, and I just can't help myself."

"Me, too," she whispered against his lips. Her hands clung to his shoulders, needing the support of them, needing the contact with his solid, powerful body. "I just can't be strong anymore. I need you, Marsh, and I'm so tired of trying to be strong."

He smiled against her lips and murmured, "Why must either of us fight something that's so good, so right for us? It's a losing battle, darling. Can't you see that?"

"Yes, but . . ."

"No buts," he said thickly as he raked his hands through her hair before finally cupping her face. "Just kiss me and let me hold you. Otherwise, I think I'll die of wanting."

"I've felt the same way," she breathed softly. She closed her eyes, succumbing to his soft, persuasive words, to the longings of her heart, and she lifted her glowing face to his. The kiss they shared was deep, soul-deep in its intensity, as it went on and on. Pam's arms went around Marsh's waist while his were around her shoulders, holding her tightly as though he would never again let her go. His mouth moved over hers hungrily and her lips parted so that their tongues could touch in fiery intimacy.

Marsh's eyes seemed to devour her face after the kiss ended. "You're inside me," he murmured, "in my system, and no matter how much I tell myself to forget you, I can't. How"—he made a throaty laugh—"can you forget something as vital to you as your own blood, your own heart or lungs?"

His arms crushed her to him again as he continued to plant feverish kisses on her cheeks, her brow, her eyelids. Pam felt him tremble against her, even as her own heart pounded so hard that it seemed to vibrate right down to her toes.

When his hand slid beneath the collar of her robe to stroke her throat, Pam shivered deliciously. Marsh bent his head to kiss the sensitive place, and she gasped with delight.

A moment later Marsh eased her to the carpet, coming down on one knee beside her. Her senses swirled dizzily at the light of passion that was so evident in his gaze. His lips sought hers again as his hands loosened her robe and shoved it away from her shoulders.

Beneath the robe Pam was wearing a creamy satin nightgown. It was exquisite and delicate, with ecru lace down the center that offered enticing glimpses of the dusky hollow between the fullness of her breasts. The soft, clinging fabric seemed to mold itself around her breasts and hips before falling in smooth folds past her knees and down to her feet.

Marsh caught his breath as he looked at her. "You're . . ." He broke off and swallowed hard. "I've never seen you more beautiful!" He slid one of the dainty straps down her shoulder so that his lips could touch the tender flesh just above the swell of her breasts. "Do you wear such an exotic nightgown every night," he asked huskily, "or did you plan to seduce me tonight?" A hint of laughter thickened his voice.

His question startled her. Why had she worn this particular gown tonight? Pam lifted her hand to his face, lovingly running a fingertip over his lips. "I suppose I must have worn it for you," she said with a flirtatious smile, "since I seldom wear it. It was a gift from a college friend."

"It had better be a female friend," Marsh growled, entirely serious.

Pam heard the jealousy in his voice and laughed. "It was a female friend," she admitted.

She felt his body relax beside her. "In that case," he said magnanimously, "she has excellent taste. Even so . . ." He stopped, and his eyes twinkled devilishly as he looked at her.

"Even so . . . what?" Pam asked, although she could easily guess what he was about to say. The glint in his eyes was a dead giveaway.

"It's a lovely gown,' ' he said, "but it'll be even lovelier off." His hand had been sliding smoothly along the satin that draped over her hip and thigh, but suddenly his hands deftly followed his words and the gown slithered up, up and over her head.

Marsh caught his breath again, sharply, and expelled it slowly as his gaze took in the sight of her uncovered body. "Words," he said gruffly, "can't begin to tell you how lovely, how magnificent, you are." He buried his face between her breasts.

Pam threaded her hands through his hair, feeling warm and desirable and something else she couldn't define. It took her a moment to realize that the unfamiliar emotion she felt was pure happiness.

Marsh's hands stroked her breasts and then his lips brought the nipples to throbbing, taut peaks. Pleasure shivered through Pam, and once again she was startled that her body had kept secret from her so many years such thrilling ecstasy. She was giddy from the feelings she was experiencing, riding high on rapture and utterly captivated by the man and the beautiful, delectable things his hands and lips were doing to her. At the same time, she wanted more, more, like a person with an unquenchable thirst.

The power of her desire brought forth a bold, wild streak from within her that stunned and gratified them both.

She pushed him away from her body so that she could unbutton his shirt. She heightened the tension for them both by pausing after each button had been opened to kiss the side of his chest that was revealed. Slowly, she worked her way down toward his belt and she felt him tense at the shock of such sudden passion.

Yet Pam wasn't finished. She removed his shirt, and

her kisses radiated outward to cover the rest of his bared chest. When he tried to reach for her, she shoved his hands away and shook her head. "No. Not yet," she whispered emphatically. She got to her knees and moved around to his back, where her lips began the sensual assault once more, beginning at his shoulders and working down.

Marsh's body trembled beneath her lips and Pam laughed softly, exultant with heady, glorious power. The delightful torture continued until she'd covered his entire back with warm, moist kisses. Then she nuzzled her face into a muscular arm.

But Marsh had had all he could withstand. He turned suddenly and captured her, pressing her tender breasts tightly against the strength of his chest before he lowered them both to the carpet again.

His eyes glittered dangerously. "There's only so much torment a man can take," he told her hoarsely, "and I've just about reached my limit of endurance."

Pam giggled.

"Ah, so now I'm an object of ridicule, am I?" He pretended to snarl and bent his head to nibble at her earlobe.

"Never." Pam turned serious as her hand rose to caress his neck. "It's just that I'm a bit delirious at the idea that I can make you want me so much," she said with a catch to her voice.

Marsh lifted his head so that he could look down at her. His dark eyes were unwavering as he asked, "Is that so astounding?"

"Yes," Pam answered, almost humbly. "To me it is."

"Why?" he asked, sounding genuinely amazed.

"Surely you must know by now that all you have to do is look at me to set me on fire for you."

Pam shook her head. "It doesn't matter," she replied in a low voice. Her hands moved sensuously over his chest, brushing the crispy dark mat of hair. "Just . . . make love to me, Marsh," she pleaded.

He needed no further urging. Quickly, Marsh shed the remainder of his clothes and then lay down to join her once more, his magnificent male physique eager for her.

Marsh pulled her on top of him, covering her face with kisses before his lips sought her lovely, rounded breasts. Pam's tender feminine curves fitted perfectly over his long, angular body and the warmth of him seemed to radiate right through her skin.

Then he flipped her over as he played yet another erotic, teasing game with her. He kissed her everywhere, even her toes, and then his lips found and tantalized her most secret places.

Just as Pam was certain she was on the brink of insanity because of the high-voltage currents of desire flashing through her, they came together and clasped their arms tightly around one another. Their love lifted them to the highest bliss a man and woman can know as they became, for a brief and beautiful eternity, one.

A little later, when their pulses had slowed and their breathing had returned to normal, they lay facing each other, smiling.

Marsh's fingers gently caressed Pam's shoulder. "How soon will you marry me, darling?" he murmured.

The warm afterglow of their lovemaking abruptly

faded for Pam. She stiffened and felt a chill climb her spine. Her smile vanished. "Marsh, I never said . . ." She broke off in distress.

His hands were still, then abandoned her shoulder. "You asked me not to go," he said in a strange tone. His eyes became sharp, gray steel. "I thought you meant you'd changed your mind, that you really wanted me."

"I did. I do." Pam said. She sighed raggedly. "Oh, Marsh, I'm so mixed up! I love you, I *do,*" she cried as she saw the open skepticism in his face, "and I don't want you to go! I don't want to lose you, but I . . . I can't marry you. Don't you see? It would only end in failure like everything else in my life, and I can't, won't bind you up in my failure. I love you too much to do that to you."

Marsh shook his head. "No," he said in a voice so cold that it froze her blood. "What you're really saying is that you don't love me enough to try to make a success of our relationship. Marriage takes more effort than you're willing to make, so you'd prefer to condemn both of us to a lifetime of loneliness rather than to try to make a go at it."

He got up and turned his back to her while he dressed with haste. Feeling wretched and so cold she was sure she would never be warm again, Pam shivered and sat up to reach for her robe. She slid her arms into it and, with trembling fingers, pulled the lapels together in the front. Her eyes were glazed with burning tears and she yearned to find the words to end the heavy tension in the room, but no words came. No matter what she said, she could never make Marsh understand what it had cost her to say no.

When he had finished dressing, Marsh turned to gaze down at her. "I made a mistake thinking if we loved enough, it would free us both from the past. But I don't think you want to be free of it. It's a convenient excuse for avoiding taking a chance on the future."

Chapter Ten

*I*t was a broiling hot Friday afternoon in late August when Pam again visited the lawyer in Natchitoches. An efficient air conditioning system refrigerated the office so that she found the temperature a comfortable, welcome respite from the heat outdoors.

The only sound in the office besides the hum of the air conditioner was the rustle of papers. The attorney, Mr. Nivens, was silent as he waited for Pam to go over the thick sheaf of legal papers he had handed her.

But Pam was no longer reading and she no longer felt comfortable. Chills made her shiver while her eyes were riveted to the page before her. Shock held her spellbound, so that for a moment she wasn't even breathing. It couldn't be. It just couldn't be!

A raspy sound came from her throat and the papers in her hand rattled again. Right on the first page was the name of the purchaser, and it leaped immediately to her attention like a glaring neon sign. Pam lifted her head and her dazed eyes met the lawyer's across the desk.

"Yes?" prompted Mr. Nivens. "You have a question?"

Her mouth was dry. Pam's tongue moistened her lips and she swallowed painfully. "The . . . the purchaser . . ." She broke off helplessly.

"Mr. Franklin." The attorney nodded. "What about him?"

Pam sucked in a deep breath, desperately needing the oxygen because her head was whirling. She briefly closed her eyes, then, opening them again, said in a rush, "I can't sell to him."

Confusion covered Mr. Nivens' face. He stared at Pam blankly, uncomprehending. "But why not? If it's his financial soundness you're worried about, I can assure you there's no reason to be concerned. I've checked out his credit rating and it is excellent. Mr. Franklin is quite wealthy, I understand."

"Is he?" Pam asked, faintly surprised. She dropped the papers back onto the polished desk and shook her head. "That doesn't matter," she said dully. "The deal is off. I can't possibly sell to him."

"But I don't understand, Mrs. Norris!" Nivens exclaimed. "What is the problem? Perhaps we can work out whatever—"

Pam shook her head again and interrupted him. "There's nothing to work out, Mr. Nivens. I'm sorry, but I can't sign those papers." She stood up.

Mr. Nivens rose also. "But . . . what am I to tell Mr.

Franklin's lawyer?" he asked anxiously. "We both expected everything to go routinely! By next week you'd have your check and Mr. Franklin would have the resort. Besides, I thought you really needed to sell. Buyers of places like yours don't just grow on trees, you know," he chided.

"I know, and I really am sorry," Pam apologized again. "Tell Mr. Franklin's attorney . . . no, don't tell him anything," she said, changing her mind in midsentence. "I'll tell Mr. Franklin myself."

The attorney looked thoroughly disapproving. "This is all highly irregular," he protested.

Pam shrugged and picked up her handbag. "Promise me you won't say a word. I don't want this to get back to Mr. Franklin until I can talk with him personally."

"You know him, then?" Mr. Nivens asked.

"Yes," Pam replied softly. "I know him well. That's why I can't allow him to do this."

It had been a month, a lifetime, since Marsh had gone away, and, despite the passing weeks, her heartache had not diminished any whatsoever. It seemed that each new day brought its own memories of him: Scotty's love affair with his treehouse; a chat with Gus at the marina; the cabin Marsh had used; the duck pond. One day in Many she'd happened to bump into Andy. They'd chatted a few minutes, but afterwards Pam could only think how much seeing him had reminded her of Marsh and his arrogant assumption from the first that she hadn't been interested in Andy. Only in him.

There were nights when she questioned the wisdom

of her decision to let Marsh go, nights when her body ached to be held in his arms, when her mind betrayed her by recalling the exquisite joy she'd felt when he'd made love to her. The day Scotty received a cheerful letter from him, she was certain she'd made a horrible mistake. Here was Marsh still being kind and thoughtful and demonstrating his fondness for Scotty even when he was far away and no longer had a real reason to continue being nice to one little boy, and Pam felt sick to think that she might have cheated Scotty out of having a wonderful father. But how could she know for sure?

Now, as she drove home from her trip to see the lawyer, she did know one thing with unshakable conviction: Marsh had no other motive for buying the resort except his love and concern for her, and no matter how hard up she was financially, she couldn't take advantage of him by allowing the sale to go through. Still, the least she owed him was her gratitude because he'd cared enough to try to solve her problems, and in the face of such unselfish love she knew she owed him something more—an explanation.

When she got home she found both Gus and Zelma in the store. Gus now ran the store for part of each day, and when he felt like it, which more and more often he did, he was beginning to take on a few of the less strenuous maintenance jobs. Since they now had the younger man to do the heavier jobs, it was an arrangement that worked out well for everyone because Gus's help in the store freed Pam and Zelma for more of the chores that had often been somewhat neglected because of a lack of time.

Pam hoped her news that she would now need to find a new buyer wasn't going to give Gus a setback, but she also knew she had to be honest. There was simply no way to cover up the matter.

When she explained who the potential new owner had been and that she couldn't allow him to buy it out of compassion for them all, she was the one who got the fresh shock.

"I told Marsh you'd probably feel this way when he first mentioned his idea to me," Gus said calmly.

Pam stared at him. "You mean you knew all along who the buyer was?"

Zelma nodded. "Of course we did. Marsh had a long talk with us about it before he called that lawyer friend of his and told him to go to work on it."

"But . . . why didn't you tell me?"

Gus shrugged. "Marsh asked us to keep quiet. He sort of hoped that if all the paperwork had already been done by the time you found out, you might be inclined to allow the sale to go through."

"You're not angry with us for not telling you, are you?" Zelma asked with concern. "Marsh made us promise."

Pam smiled wanly. "No. He asked you not to say anything, so you didn't. But I can't let Marsh buy this place merely because I'm in a jam."

"Have you called and told him yet?" Gus asked.

Pam shook her head. "No. I'm not going to call. I'm going to see him. It's better if we work this thing out in person. If I go tomorrow, will you keep Scotty for me? I'll probably get a motel room and stay overnight."

"No problem," Zelma said.

She turned away, and Pam was unable to see her smile of satisfaction.

It was gloomy the next day as Pam headed east, and before long it began to rain, slowly and steadily. The gray day and the constant rain reminded her again of Marsh and the day they'd discovered those children adrift in their boat. That evening they had made love.

She tried to concentrate on something else; thinking of the good times would get her nowhere, and she had to concentrate on her driving, what she would say to Marsh once she saw him and, when it was over, the fact that she must forget him for good.

It was after one o'clock by the time she reached Metarie, the suburb of New Orleans where Marsh lived. The rain was lashing down viciously, making driving hazardous and nerve-wracking, and when she got off the freeway Pam could scarcely read street signs because of the heavy downpour.

She found a shopping center and stopped there, dashing through the rain to run inside, where she first bought a local map and then found a cafeteria where she could eat lunch while she studied the best route to take to the condominium where Marsh lived.

By now she was so tense, both from the rain and the upcoming interview with Marsh, that her stomach was in knots and she could scarcely eat a bite of the food she ordered. Perhaps it had been a mistake to come after all. What good would it do to tell Marsh the things she had come to say? The only thing it could do would be help Marsh to understand her a little better. It wouldn't change anything between them.

But she had come this far and she wasn't going to turn back like a coward now. Deep inside, she knew there was another, even more important reason for sticking to her course. It would give her the opportunity to see Marsh one last time, before she put him altogether in her past. It was selfish, foolishly indulgent, but she couldn't help herself.

Resolutely, she rose and threaded her way between the tables and went toward the cashier's desk. A few minutes later she was outside again and grateful that the rain had slackened considerably, although the sky was still dark and heavy with moisture.

Shortly after two-thirty that Saturday afternoon, Pam stood outside the door to Marsh's apartment. She removed her scarf and raincoat and smoothed her hair before nervously tugging at the bottom of her crochet-knit top that overlapped her beige slacks. When there was no further excuse to delay, she rang the doorbell at last.

The door opened almost immediately, but the man who stood there wasn't Marsh. He appeared to be a few years older, slightly shorter, and his hair wasn't quite so dark, but his resemblance to Marsh was unmistakable.

Pam was so taken aback to find someone else there, something she never calculated when she set out on her impromptu journey, that for a moment she couldn't speak. Yet the man was looking at her and she had to say something.

"Hello," she said at last. "I was l–looking for Marsh Franklin. Is he . . . ?"

"Sure, he's here," the other man said. He smiled

warmly and touched her arm, urging her forward. "Come in, come in. Marsh is so secretive. He never told us he'd invited such a beautiful guest."

"But he didn't . . ." Pam began, but by then she had already been pulled into the room, and the rest of her words died in her throat as she stared around in dismay. The living room was crowded with people, wall-to-wall with people, and she realized she had inadvertently crashed a party. Color surged to her face as all eyes trained upon her, and she wished the floor would open up and swallow her. Talk about bad timing!

"I'm Jim Franklin, Marsh's brother," the man beside her said. "And your name?"

"Pamela. Pamela Norris," she replied automatically. She hadn't seen Marsh anywhere in the crowd. "Perhaps I'd better go. I had no idea Marsh was having a party." She half turned toward the door, but the man's hand closed around her arm, stopping her.

"Nonsense. I'm sure he'll be delighted to have you here to help celebrate his birthday." He turned his head and shouted, "Hey, Marsh, come out here! We've got a surprise for you!" To Pam he added in a normal tone, "He's in the kitchen with Mom."

"What is it?" Marsh asked as he came out of the kitchen, holding a large spoon. "I'm busy supervising Mom to make sure she puts enough shrimp into the gumbo and—"

He never finished the sentence. Marsh looked across the room and saw Pam standing near the door, and suddenly he couldn't swallow. He could scarcely believe his eyes.

A pain that had frozen his heart for the past month

suddenly melted as a wild elation took its place. Pam, his beautiful Pam, was really here!

A few long strides carried Marsh across the floor and when he reached her, he didn't hesitate. He pulled her into his arms, oblivious to the others in the room, never hearing their stunned murmurs as he bent his head and kissed Pam with utter starvation.

When he released her at last, her face was flushed and an odd shyness lurked in her blue eyes. Only then did Marsh remember their audience. He chuckled softly and whispered in her ear, "Sorry, darling. I got carried away and forgot we weren't alone. I'm so glad to see you."

"Marsh," Pam said in a low, urgent voice, "I never dreamed you were having a party. I didn't mean to intrude."

"Are you kidding?" he exclaimed. "You just *made* the party." With his arm firmly around her waist, he turned her toward the others and said aloud, "Let me introduce you to my family."

A few minutes later she had met everyone, including Marsh's other two brothers, Dave and Tom, all their wives and children, and his parents. Pam's head swirled from so many names and faces and she was so hopelessly confused she was certain she would never get them all straightened out. Had Melissa been Tom's wife or was that Jim's daughter's name?

Marsh smiled in sympathy. "Don't worry," he told her. "There's so many of us, no one expects you to remember their name right away."

"Just say 'hey you,' " Dave teased, "and any of us will answer."

"Can I get you a glass of wine?"

"Come sit here. We'll make space for you."

"I hope you like gumbo," Marsh's mother said with a gentle smile.

"I love it," Pam said shyly, "but I didn't come to eat. Besides, I just had lunch."

"Then you'd better develop a fresh appetite," Marsh said with a twinkle in his eyes. "Mom makes the best gumbo in all of New Orleans." He sat down beside her on the sofa. "I wish you had brought Scotty with you. How is he?"

"He's fine. He misses you," she said with honesty.

"I've missed him, too. And Gus? How is he?"

"Doing wonderfully. He and Zelma send their love."

The word hung there between them for a long, intense moment, and again the room blurred, the other guests faded, and they were only aware of each other. But then Marsh, with an effort to keep his voice casual, turned toward his father and said, "Dad, ask Pam to show you a picture of her son. You'd like Scotty. He's a baseball fan, too."

The afternoon passed pleasantly, and Pam was amazed to discover how much she enjoyed herself. Marsh's family did their utmost to make her feel welcome. The food was delicious and she found she had a healthy appetite for the meal Mrs. Franklin had prepared. She even enjoyed watching Marsh open his gifts, though she felt bad because she hadn't known to bring one herself. But when she mentioned it, Marsh brushed her concerns aside.

"How could you know?" he asked reasonably. "Besides, your being here is a gift."

His words should have warmed her, but instead they brought a new dread. Marsh assumed she had come to end the estrangement between them. It was obvious from his initial greeting and the way he had remained constantly at her side all afternoon, more often than not with a possessive arm around her waist. Louder than words he had boldly proclaimed his love for her for all his family to see, and she had not known what to do to counter it. Later, when the party began to break up and Marsh's relatives were leaving, they bid her very cordial good-byes in a manner that left her in no doubt that, not only did they expect to see her again, they already practically considered her part of the family.

When everyone had gone at last, Pam went to stand at a window and gazed out. It was still raining and early darkness had fallen.

Marsh came up behind her and slid both arms around her waist, pulling her back to lean against his tall, angular frame. His arms and his face pressed next to her cheek were warm, but inside Pam went cold. The afternoon had been fun, a time out of reality, but now reality had returned and could no longer be avoided.

"I need to leave soon," she said softly. "I have to find a motel room before it gets too late."

"Don't be silly," Marsh said gruffly. "You'll stay here with me tonight."

"Marsh . . ." Pam hesitated, wondering how best to start. Gently, she disengaged herself from his arms and turned to face him. Her eyes were dark and serious. "Marsh, I didn't come for the reason you think."

"No?" Pam felt wretched as the light died in his eyes, leaving them a dreary gray like the day itself had been. "Why did you come?"

She sighed and, to avoid his eyes, turned toward the window again. "Yesterday I saw the lawyer. Saw your name on the papers. Until then I had no idea you were the party who wanted to buy the resort. I came to tell you that while I'm very, very grateful for what you were trying to do for me, I can't let you do it."

"Leave gratitude out of it and of course you can sell to me. It's strictly a business deal. I don't come with the package."

There was bitterness in his voice that Pam knew came from the rebuff she'd just delivered to him, and an ache welled up inside her. She hadn't meant to do it, but she'd hurt Marsh yet again.

She turned back to him, restraining herself with difficulty from reaching out to touch the hard, firm jaw, to soften his lips with her kisses. She didn't dare, because if she did she would be lost. "It's not strictly a business deal, and we both know it," she told him. "It's just one more example of your generosity. I appreciate it, Marsh, I honestly do, but I will not use you this way. If I lose the place, then I lose it, but I won't allow you to be a part of my failure."

"Failure!" Marsh exclaimed with exasperation. "You've talked about that before. You've got some sort of hang-up about it that I just don't understand!"

"I know you don't," she admitted softly. "And maybe it's time you did."

Pam walked across the room and sank into a chair. Her legs were so weak she didn't think they could hold her much longer. When Marsh followed and sat down on the sofa opposite her, she glanced away toward a bookshelf. She could think better if she didn't look at him.

"My marriage was a disaster from start to finish," she began in a lifeless voice. "I was so young and I thought it was love. When we were going together Mike was attentive and thoughtful and I seemed to be the most important thing in his life. I . . . I needed that. I'd never really felt important to either of my parents. First they had each other and their constant fights, and after their divorce they always seemed more interested in other people than in me. Anyway, I married Mike, determined that no matter what it took, it would last, would be a success." She shook her head and said more to herself than to him, "In a way, Mike did me a favor walking out on me the way he finally did, because I probably would never have gotten up the courage to get out of the marriage otherwise. But then, I had no means to do it."

Her gaze flickered to Marsh's grave, attentive face, then down to her hands. "There were always other women for him, almost from the very first, even before he left me to move in with his latest girl friend. I was . . . I was a disappointment to him sexually. He said I was frigid."

Marsh uttered a gutteral sound. "It's not true!" he exploded.

Pam managed a wan, grateful smile as she glanced briefly at him once again. "I know that now," she whispered softly. She cleared her throat and continued.

"I believed it, then, however. So that was just one of the problems, one of Mike's dissatisfactions with me. But there were others, too. I tried so hard to please him, but I rarely did. My housekeeping wasn't spotless enough to suit him, my cooking wasn't how he wanted it done, or it was served at the wrong time. He was always criticizing, endlessly finding fault with everything. He even humiliated me in front of guests sometimes," she added, choking over the memories.

"Why did you put up with it?" Marsh asked angrily. "I know you wanted to keep your marriage intact, but nobody should have to take that sort of abuse!"

"I was a doormat, Marsh!" Pam cried angrily. "A pushover. Don't you see? I was foolish enough from the very beginning to knuckle under just to keep the peace that in a way it was as much my fault as his, because I allowed him to get by with it! I keep wondering if I'd done more to please him, if we could have made it. Or if I'd stood up for myself, maybe then he would have loved me and I could have loved myself as well." Tears came to her eyes and, annoyed, she brushed them away fiercely.

"None of that even sounds like you . . . like the woman I know," Marsh said wonderingly. "Pam, I . . ."

"Let me finish," she interrupted hoarsely. "There was another, even more important reason why I stayed with him. I had no money of my own with which to leave, and it's rather hard," she laughed harshly, "to be independent when you don't have a cent. I was ashamed to tell my dad how things really were, and anyway he didn't have much money either. After he died there was nothing left after all his debts had been settled."

"Couldn't you have tucked some away here and there until you'd saved enough?"

Pam shook her head. "You don't understand. The checking and savings accounts were only in Mike's name. He gave me a cash allowance for household expenses, but once a week he went over the receipts, and what I hadn't used I had to give back to him. Can you imagine that in this day and time? I had to account for every penny I ever spent, right down to each tube of lipstick or pair of pantyhose. It . . . it's so degrading not to be trusted with money, to be treated like an incompetent imbecile! The day he walked out on me," she added in a dull recital of fact, "he left me a hundred dollars and nothing more!"

"The bastard!" Marsh muttered.

Pam was so wrapped up in that unhappy time that she scarcely heard him. "Mike was furious when I became pregnant with Scotty. He never wanted him, and on the night I went into labor, a neighbor had to drive me to the hospital. Mike was out only God knows where. He didn't show up at the hospital until the next afternoon. I had just given birth to his son but he didn't so much as bring me a single flower or visit the nursery to see the baby," she said sadly. "He only complained about how much the hospital stay was costing."

"Pam." The word was an anguished sound.

Pam's eyes were glazed as she stared at the bookshelf again. "I was devastated when he left me. Not because

I had any more illusions about loving him, but because I was scared and didn't know what to do next. At least while we were together I'd had a roof over Scotty and my heads and food on the table. Mike had never allowed me to take a job because his pride forbade it; so there I was with no marketable skills and a nine-month-old baby to support. I knew that once it reached the courts they would force Mike to give me child support, but in the meantime I had no money. By then both my parents were dead and I had no one."

"Your Uncle Bob?" Marsh asked.

Pam nodded. "The first month after Mike left, I was absolutely panic-stricken. While a neighbor cared for Scotty, I searched for a job, with no luck. The money soon ran out and if it hadn't been for my neighbor, the baby and I would literally have gone hungry. She saw to it that we had food, but we both knew that couldn't continue indefinitely. Mike never called or came by after he left us, and I didn't know where he was living. I tried to call him at his office, to ask him for more money, but he had quit his job and nobody there knew where he was. I was on my own completely and I had to do something. Finally, I remembered Uncle Bob. I had only met him once, the year before when he had come to Chicago for my dad's funeral. I hated to ask him for help, because he was virtually a stranger, but, God bless his soul, he took us under his wing immediately. He wired money for plane fare and Scotty and I came to live with him in Louisiana. A few months later Mike died in a motorcycle accident and what money he'd had came to me. I used part of it to attend college and the rest is in a trust fund for Scotty."

"Pam." Marsh's voice was husky as he came to kneel beside her chair. He took her cold hands in his. "Darling, I'm sorry. I had no idea it had been like that."

Pam went on in the same dull tone. "I swore to myself that I would never again give any man such power over my life. And I won't, Marsh. Not even for you."

"But I'm not like Mike!" he exclaimed. "I'm not him, Pam, and I'm damned sure not on any power trip! I don't want control over you! I only want to love you!"

She shook her head. "People think they're in love," she said sorrowfully, "but after they marry, things change. I failed Mike. I couldn't live up to his expectations and he couldn't be happy with me, and so his love died."

"Face it, Pam," Marsh snapped angrily. "He was a selfish man who didn't love anything at all beyond himself and his role of tyrant! He got away with it by making it damned near impossible for you to leave him, and yet when he felt like leaving himself, he walked out without a backward glance, much less concern about where Scotty and your next meal was coming from! You can't dignify the way he treated you with the word love. And how can you possibly allow him to still have the power to make you think you failed *him?* Or that you would necessarily fail with me or any other man? Look at me, Pam!"

When she finally did, the piercing intensity of his gaze held her own, mesmerizing her so that she couldn't look away. His eyes were dark fire, burning with the strength of his emotions, and his hands tightened over hers, his heat radiating into her.

"You saw my parents today," he said. "My brothers and their wives. They're all still in love. So are Gus and Zelma. There's a sharing between them. They've all worked and pulled together to make their marriages successful. There's not a dominant–submissive relationship in the bunch that I can tell. They're all partnerships, and that's what marriage should be."

"Yes, it is what it should be," she answered, "but mine wasn't, and I'm terrified to try again. I've struggled hard to be independent, Marsh, and the freedom to be my own person, to make my own decisions is something I simply can't give up. Not ever."

Abruptly, Marsh dropped her hands and rose. He paced the room like a caged lion before finally stopping in front of her, feet spread apart, hands on his hips. He laughed, and it was humorless.

"My wife, Lynn, was just the opposite of you. She was too possessive, to the point where I felt smothered by her. Unlike your Mike, I gave her unlimited access to my income, but though she dearly loved to spend my money, most of the time she wanted me there with her while she did it, approving her every purchase as though she couldn't trust her own judgment when it came to a pair of blasted shoes! Have you ever stopped to think how exasperating that can be to most husbands? *I* have no desire to make a decision on every dress my wife buys!" He shook his head. "She was jealous of everything connected with my life—my relationship with my family, my work, my friends. Sometimes she would call me at work three or four times a day, for no real reason. It drove me crazy! And if I was so much as ten minutes late getting home from the office at night, she would be in tears, accusing me of infidelity. She didn't want children and she only endured sex. So next"—he drew in a deep breath and laughed again, harshly—"I got engaged to a woman who also was too possessive in a different way. She liked my money and my success and she wanted to push me to the top of the social directory whether I wanted to be there or not. In the meantime, though, fidelity meant nothing at all to her."

"I'm sorry," Pam said in a hushed voice. "You . . . you've been hurt badly, too."

"Yes, I have." Marsh's eyes glinted. "But I haven't let it embitter me the way it has you." He sighed. "I want you, Pam. To be married to you, to have children with you and to be a father to Scotty, to build a life together and to grow old with you. I want to sleep in the same bed with you every night for the rest of my life with neither of us ever having to worry about not trusting the other. I want to share my money with you, my heartaches and my joys with you, and I want you to give the same back to me. I want you to be my confidante and my best friend; I want to fight with you and make love with you and I want to be there when your hair turns gray and the spring in your step slows down. If that's possession, then yes, I want to possess you for as long as we both live. But I don't want to rob you of your spirit any more than I want you to rob me of mine. Isn't it just possible that we can find a freedom together that's better than what we've each had alone?"

Pam didn't reply and, after waiting for a long time for her to speak, Marsh turned in defeat and left the room. He had said everything he felt in his heart, and yet it still wasn't enough. Pam couldn't trust in his love and there was nothing more left for him to say.

He went into his bedroom and closed the door. She could let herself out of the apartment. He couldn't bear to watch her leave.

Marsh didn't bother to turn on the light. He went around the bed and sank down on the edge of it, gazing at the dark windowpanes. Rain beat upon the glass, echoing the pain inside of him.

He'd been indescribably happy when he'd seen Pam standing there in his living room today. He supposed because it was what he'd wanted to believe, he'd instantly leapt to the conclusion that she had come to him to make things up, to end their loneliness, to tell him she'd changed her mind and wanted to marry him.

Fool! he now told himself savagely. *Fool!* Marsh buried his face in his hands. When he'd seen her, he had completely forgotten that Gene was negotiating with her lawyer for the resort; he'd forgotten their differences, her fears, his anger and hurt. He'd forgotten everything except how much she meant to him and how glad he was to see her and how proud he was to be able to show her off to his family.

Marsh sniffed with self-derision. His family was certainly going to think he'd gone mad, behaving the

way he had today about a woman who didn't want him.
He had openly let them see his love because he had
genuinely thought Pam had come to him for good.

Pam didn't know how long she sat unmoving in the
quiet living room. Ten minutes? An hour? She knew
that Marsh had long ago given up and that he expected
her to leave, yet she couldn't seem to bring herself to
do it. She felt numb, washed out, lifeless, and she
wasn't sure her legs would support her if she attempted
to stand up.

For the first time since her arrival this afternoon, she
looked around the room, really seeing it. The sofa and
chairs were a camel-colored tweed, the tables and
bookcase a rich dark brown. A large, beautiful painting
of a bayou scene with moss-draped cypress trees and a
lone fisherman in a pirogue dominated the wall behind
the sofa; on another wall were photographs of all sizes.
A wooden, hand-carved heron stood, one leg folded,
on the coffee table. It was a tasteful room, a man's
room, masculine and uncluttered and straightforward
in honest beauty.

Straightforward and honest, like Marsh himself, she
thought abruptly. *I don't want control over you,* he'd
said. *I only want to love you.* When had Marsh ever lied
to her? From the beginning, from the first moment they
met he'd been open about his attraction to her, about
his fondness for Scotty, about his growing love for her.
Marsh might have his faults, but dishonesty wasn't
among them.

Pam rose and, as though a magnet drew her, she

went to study the photographs grouped on the opposite wall. There were snapshots of Marsh and his brothers when they were youngsters, of his parents, of his brothers and their wives on their wedding days, of his nieces and nephews at various stages from babyhood to school pictures.

Family very clearly meant the world to Marsh. If she searched forever, Pam knew she could never find a better father for Scotty. Marsh and her son shared a special relationship between them that was separate from either of their feelings for her. They had the kind of friendship and love between them that would last a lifetime, whether she married Marsh or not.

Marsh's ex-wife had denied him a family of his own. That must have been as hard for him to bear as Mike's rejection of Scotty had been for her. When she'd first married him, she'd had rosy dreams of having a large family.

She could give Marsh the children he wanted, she thought suddenly. A warm, sweet feeling stole over her at the idea of having more children; Marsh's children. It was so easy to imagine Scotty and his younger brothers and sisters involved in the Franklin family celebrations. She could envision the total, delightful chaos of it all, the way it had been today, with children running around playing and laughing while their parents compared notes on child-rearing and probably exchanging outgrown hand-me-downs. What fun it could be . . . the sort of life neither she nor Scotty had ever known.

But she couldn't base her decision on family. Marriage was more than that. It was the relationship between herself and Marsh that had to be the deciding factor.

There was no comparison between Mike and Marsh. Mike had been selfish, a tightwad, super-critical. With sudden insight Pam realized he'd been unhappy with himself and had projected it onto her. She had believed herself a failure sexually because Mike had told her so, yet Marsh had already proved differently. So wasn't it possible that all his other criticisms had been no more valid? Mike hadn't wanted children, but Marsh already loved the son that wasn't his own. And Marsh respected her as a person in her own right. He hadn't condemned her as stupid or unfit to handle money because she'd had problems with the resort; instead, he'd tried to help her. He was kind and generous and giving. Life with Marsh could never be the way it had been with Mike. His generosity came from the soul, not just his pocketbook. Mike had had none at all.

So by what right did she have to project her *own* unhappy fears of the past onto a man like Marsh, and make them both desperately miserable in the bargain? The realization that that was what she had been doing shocked Pam and made her suddenly furious with herself.

Abruptly, she whirled and hurried down the hall to Marsh's closed bedroom door. When she opened it, she found the room in darkness. Marsh sat on the bed facing the window, his shadowy back to her and his posture one of abject despair.

She saw him tense as he realized she was there.

"Haven't you gone yet?" he asked gruffly, without turning.

Pam cleared her throat. "If . . . if you can find it in your heart to forgive me for all my doubts and fears," she begged in a thick voice, "I'd like to stay forever."

Marsh turned as she went around the bed and sat down beside him. Now that she was close, she saw how haggard his face was—again, her fault. "What did you say?" he asked in a strange, distant voice.

Pam touched his hand and he started, as though he were going to pull away, but then he didn't. Heartened, she said softly, "You said you weren't Mike, that you weren't like him. It . . . it took a while for that to sink in. Oh, not your words," she went on, "but the real truth of it. You're as different from him in every way possible as can be. You've shown me and *shown* me that you truly love me, but I was too blinded by fear to really see. I'm sorry for that, Marsh. If it's not too late, if you'll still have me, I'd like very much to be your wife."

"Why?" The question was harsh and blunt, but the sudden softening in his eyes betrayed him.

Pam laughed gently, and in a bold, sensual movement of her hands, she ran them over his chest, opening a button on his shirt so that she could thrust her fingers inside to touch his warm skin. Beneath her hand, she could feel the strong, steady beat of his heart.

Her eyes went dreamy. "Because I want to see you teaching Scotty how to shave and to drive a car; I want to watch you puff with pride as you walk our daughter down the aisle on her wedding day; and I want to be around to see what a crotchety old man you become forty years down the road."

"Is that all?" he asked. His gaze never left her face.

She shook her head. "No. I want to be part of that boisterous family that was here earlier today, and marrying you is the only way I can accomplish that. Do they have birthday parties like that for every member of the family?" she asked in awed wistfulness, thinking how many of them there were.

Marsh nodded. "Every single one," he told her. "Of course, on the months when more than one has a birthday or an anniversary, we combine the parties. The family's getting so large we'd be partying full-time if we didn't try to hold it down just a little. So you liked them, did you?" He was smiling now, and he lifted her free hand to his lips. "Are they the only other reason you want to marry me?"

Pam shook her head again and became serious. "There are a lot of good, sensible reasons to marry you," she said quietly. "You're good to Scotty, you're kind and generous, you have a great sense of humor and can be a lot of fun, and you're so good-looking I'll always be the envy of other women. But Marsh, the real reason I want to marry you is because I love you and all I can see is an empty, bleak future without you. I want the things you said earlier. I want to fight with you and make love with you, too. I want to try to find that freedom together that you talked about," she ended huskily.

Marsh's arms encircled her. "We'll have it," he promised softly. "As long as we love each other, we'll have it. I'll never try to stifle you, Pam, or make you

feel inadequate. Growing into our potential and accepting and meeting challenges is what life's all about, and I
would never try to hold you down from becoming the
best of yourself."

His words brought a lump to her throat, and it was a
moment before she could speak. "I know that," she
said at last. "When I realized that, the fear went away.
You're a strong man, Marsh, strong enough in your
own self-esteem not to feel threatened by my need for
mine. But I love you for saying it."

Marsh bent his head and kissed her, and it was a
gentle seal to their commitment to each other. When it
ended, he asked, "When will you marry me?"

Pam's eyes were shining with her love as she replied
promptly, "As soon as we get the license. I don't want
to ever be without you again, Marsh. This past month
taught me that."

"That's my girl," Marsh said approvingly. His lips
played with the corners of her lips.

"We'll be moving here, won't we?" Pam asked a
moment later. "Scotty and I?"

"I think so. Though we can discuss moving my
practice to Natchitoches if that's what you'd prefer. My
friend Gene is looking for a new partner, and that way
we could live at the resort."

Pam shook her head. "Your practice is established
here," she said thoughtfully. "And your family's here. I
think I'll rather like living near them."

"Then that's settled," Marsh said. "However, you'll
keep the resort and you won't be stubborn about letting
me put the necessary money into it to get it back up to
par. Gus and Zelma can run it while they train the new

man and hire others to help. And," he added with a pleased smile, "I think we ought to buy that bit of land from Gus and build a house there. A place to go for weekends and vacations until we retire and can move there permanently."

"Why there particularly?" Pam asked as her hands clasped around his neck.

"So we'll always have our own little corner of heaven," Marsh told her. "A place to get away from the rest of the world and just be alone together."

Pam sighed. "I'm in heaven already just being here with you."

Marsh's eyes were suddenly twinkling. "I'm not there," he said. "Yet." He pressed her down against the pillows and the glitter in his eyes changed to flames of passion.

Pam smiled her happiness and pulled him down beside her. "Then we'll make that journey together," she told him huskily.

Silhouette Special Edition

MORE ROMANCE FOR
A SPECIAL WAY TO RELAX

$2.25 each

79 ☐ Hastings	105 ☐ Sinclair	131 ☐ Lee	157 ☐ Taylor
80 ☐ Douglass	106 ☐ John	132 ☐ Dailey	158 ☐ Charles
81 ☐ Thornton	107 ☐ Ross	133 ☐ Douglass	159 ☐ Camp
82 ☐ McKenna	108 ☐ Stephens	134 ☐ Ripy	160 ☐ Wisdom
83 ☐ Major	109 ☐ Beckman	135 ☐ Seger	161 ☐ Stanford
84 ☐ Stephens	110 ☐ Browning	136 ☐ Scott	162 ☐ Roberts
85 ☐ Beckman	111 ☐ Thorne	137 ☐ Parker	163 ☐ Halston
86 ☐ Halston	112 ☐ Belmont	138 ☐ Thornton	164 ☐ Ripy
87 ☐ Dixon	113 ☐ Camp	139 ☐ Halston	165 ☐ Lee
88 ☐ Saxon	114 ☐ Ripy	140 ☐ Sinclair	166 ☐ John
89 ☐ Meriwether	115 ☐ Halston	141 ☐ Saxon	167 ☐ Hurley
90 ☐ Justin	116 ☐ Roberts	142 ☐ Bergen	168 ☐ Thornton
91 ☐ Stanford	117 ☐ Converse	143 ☐ Bright	169 ☐ Beckman
92 ☐ Hamilton	118 ☐ Jackson	144 ☐ Meriwether	170 ☐ Paige
93 ☐ Lacey	119 ☐ Langan	145 ☐ Wallace	171 ☐ Gray
94 ☐ Barrie	120 ☐ Dixon	146 ☐ Thornton	172 ☐ Hamilton
95 ☐ Doyle	121 ☐ Shaw	147 ☐ Dalton	173 ☐ Belmont
96 ☐ Baxter	122 ☐ Walker	148 ☐ Gordon	174 ☐ Dixon
97 ☐ Shaw	123 ☐ Douglass	149 ☐ Claire	175 ☐ Roberts
98 ☐ Hurley	124 ☐ Mikels	150 ☐ Dailey	176 ☐ Walker
99 ☐ Dixon	125 ☐ Cates	151 ☐ Shaw	177 ☐ Howard
100 ☐ Roberts	126 ☐ Wildman	152 ☐ Adams	178 ☐ Bishop
101 ☐ Bergen	127 ☐ Taylor	153 ☐ Sinclair	179 ☐ Meriwether
102 ☐ Wallace	128 ☐ Macomber	154 ☐ Malek	180 ☐ Jackson
103 ☐ Taylor	129 ☐ Rowe	155 ☐ Lacey	181 ☐ Browning
104 ☐ Wallace	130 ☐ Carr	156 ☐ Hastings	182 ☐ Thornton

Silhouette Special Edition

$2.25 each

183 ☐ Sinclair	190 ☐ Wisdom	197 ☐ Lind	204 ☐ Eagle
184 ☐ Daniels	191 ☐ Hardy	198 ☐ Bishop	205 ☐ Browning
185 ☐ Gordon	192 ☐ Taylor	199 ☐ Roberts	206 ☐ Hamilton
186 ☐ Scott	193 ☐ John	200 ☐ Milan	207 ☐ Roszel
187 ☐ Stanford	194 ☐ Jackson	201 ☐ Dalton	208 ☐ Sinclair
188 ☐ Lacey	195 ☐ Griffin	202 ☐ Thornton	209 ☐ Ripy
189 ☐ Ripy	196 ☐ Cates	203 ☐ Parker	210 ☐ Stanford

Silhouette Special Edition

-Coming Next Month-

A COMMON HERITAGE
by Carole Halston

•

NASHVILLE BLUES
by Patti Beckman

•

FETTERS OF THE PAST
by Laurey Bright

•

PERFECT HARMONY
by Fran Bergen

•

PIRATE'S GOLD
by Lisa Jackson

•

YOUR CHEATING HEART
by Pamela Foxe